D1515008

JOHN HAYTHORNE

The Strelsau Dimension

QUARTET CRIME

First published by Quartet Books Limited 1981
A member of the Namara Group
27 Goodge Street, London W1P 1FD

ISBN 0 7043 2285 4

Phototypeset by BSC Typesetting, London
Printed and bound in Great Britain by
Redwood Burn Limited, Trowbridge and Esher

THE STRELSAU DIMENSION

'Help!' I shouted. 'Help!'

It was the wrong way to react of course. When confronted by any savage creature, the only hope is to will oneself to remain magnificently calm. Everyone knows that. I had been often so advised in my early days when teaching briefly at a preparatory school for rather rough boys. That was before joining the more refined atmosphere of the British Diplomatic Service. 'Don't let the brutes see you're afraid. They can smell fear. Just stare them in the eye and they'll slink away.' Well, it hadn't worked with schoolboys. And I was far from certain now that it would be effective with dogs. My reflex actions took over and I heard myself yelling.

The situation would have daunted the most intrepid. And I make no pretensions to being the heroic type. The path across the park was long and lonely. The rhododendron bushes loomed thick and sinister. The treacherous sunlight of early summer was beginning to fail. I had already started to quicken my step, anxious to reach the security of the main gates where I would rejoin the Foreign Office car. I heard howling and then suddenly this ghastly pack of dogs dashed out at me. There were four or five of them at least, each lean and voracious. Alsatians presumably. If they were dogs at all! Was it legal to keep wolves in England? Almost anything might be permissible on private property. Had the Brigadier known of the danger and sent me coldbloodedly to my doom? It was a chilling thought.

The beasts frisked around me, sniffing at my hands and legs, slobbering in sinister anticipation. It was only a matter of seconds now before they started jumping up on me. Where would they take the first nip? I am an imaginative man and I could visualize only too well the sensation of canine teeth

1

being thrust through tweed and into shrinking flesh. They would have me down in an instant. Bestial breath would pour over my face and the eyes that met mine would be small and inhuman.

'Is there anyone here?' I yelled hopelessly.

It seemed such a silly way to go. I should be regarded as a tragic loss to British diplomacy. My dear mother and aunt would never be quite the same again. Several girls would mourn secretly. Since I had unfortunately not yet received the C.M.G., there could be no memorial service in the chapel of Saints Michael and George in Saint Paul's cathedral. The obituaries in the newspapers would sound distinctly flat. For a professional diplomat who had faced for years the hazards of overseas service in a dangerous world, it would seem a distinct come-down to be fatally mauled in the home counties, so near to Hayward's Heath. I am fond of laughter, but not at my own expense.

That unfortunately is what I now heard. A peal of merry but mocking laughter sounded distinctly from one of the neighbouring bushes. Then two people appeared, a girl and a young man. Even in my distress I could not help noticing that they had the same long nose and red hair as the Brigadier. The girl stepped forward and spoke crisply.

'Down, Waldemar,' she commanded. 'And you too, Wotan, silly boy.'

The dogs obediently subsided. I watched with relief, not unmixed with chagrin.

'They're quite harmless,' explained the girl. 'In fact they're all rather sweet. Just so long as you're not afraid of them.'

'I was hardly to know that,' I replied, with a touch of asperity. 'They look remarkably dangerous to me. What exactly are they?'

'Ruritanian wolf hounds,' answered the boy. 'Specially bred for hunting in the mountains. A rarity in this country.'

'No wonder,' I commented acidly. I had begun to recover my composure. That youthful laughter had been quite uncalled for.

'We ought to introduce ourselves,' said the girl mildly. 'I am Flavia Rassendyll. And this is my brother Henry.'

Her smile, though saucy, was far from unattractive. I gave her one of my more charming glances.

2

'My name is Oliver Mandrake,' I said with simple dignity. 'From the Foreign Office.'

It had all started in the spring. My departure from Washington D.C. had been little short of a disaster. It had been such a delightful post, with plenty of eager girls only too keen to minister to the needs of mature bachelors like myself. Little did I know that an architectural quirk would prove to be my ruin.

'What on earth are you doing, Oliver?' asked a rich voice in my ear. It belonged, I noted wanly, to my Ambassadress. Lady Baxendale was of commanding proportions and demeanour.

'I was just rocking the pillar,' I said weakly. It may not be generally known that in the noble British Embassy residence in Washington, designed by Sir Edward Lutyens, there is a dummy pillar, not supporting the roof, which can be rocked backwards and forwards. It usually causes a mild sensation which is not easily explained. We diplomatists like to preserve our secrets.

'I would rather you did not do that,' snapped Lady Baxendale. 'Our American friends are quite susceptible. It could cause a panic. The last thing one wants at the Queen's birthday party.'

'Eyeless in Gaza,' I retorted, 'At the mill with slaves.'

Lady Baxendale is not a cultivated person. Otherwise she would surely have recognized my Miltonic reference to poor old Samson, another prominent society figure who shook pillars with devastating effect.

'You're drunk,' snapped the Ambassadress. It was a difficult charge to disprove. Sir Horace was not normally a generous host and I had taken advantage of the special opportunity to sample deeply his Californian champagne. There is no point in belonging to the Diplomatic Service if you do not avail yourself of the occasional perks.

'If I have freely imbibed,' I countered with dignity, 'it was to sustain me against the extreme boredom of this occasion.'

A rather set look appeared on Lady Baxendale's manly countenance. With a snap of the fingers, she summoned one of her familiars, a spineless Second Secretary in the Chancery called Angus Methven.

'Please escort Mr Mandrake to the front door,' she commanded with an imperial gesture.

At that point I am alleged to have used a distinctly rude and undiplomatic phrase. Of course I deny it. My sense of self-preservation in these matters is usually acute. But against my unsupported word was that of Lady Baxendale and the unspeakable Methven. The Foreign and Commonwealth Office have a tiresome habit of believing ambassadresses. I left Washington rather quickly after that.

'You have indeed made a mess of things,' commented Lorenzo Fontwell, our burly Head of Personnel.

'It might have happened to anyone,' I replied weakly.

'Possibly,' countered Fontwell, 'but it seems to happen particularly often to you, my dear Oliver.'

He lightly sketched in my past career. Admittedly it contained a number of such abrupt departures. There was that tiresome business in Warsaw. Not to mention Lisbon. I suppose I do not suffer fools gladly. It has been a most damaging aspect of my career. Other people with far less talent and charm have forged ahead, as my dear aunt frequently points out.

'What on earth are we to do with you?' asked the personnel chief glumly.

"Another foreign posting maybe?' I suggested hopefully. 'Paris perhaps. Or Rome.'

'Quite out of the question, I'm afraid. Lady Baxendale will have written round to her chums. You'll be a marked man. What about a small consulate in central America?'

'I couldn't take anywhere too tropical. My prickly heat, you know. I have a medical certificate.'

'Then it will have to be a special mission.'

'That sounds rather exciting.'

'Sir Edmund Byfield has asked for a spare man.'

'That doesn't seem a very flattering description,' I commented ruefully. 'But I suppose it's one better than being a loose woman.'

4

'Well, it isn't exactly easy to place you. Byfield often has amusing ideas up his sleeve. If you do well for him, the Board will take an altogether rosier view of your prospects.'

Sir Edmund Byfield, a former Ambassador and a Deputy Under-Secretary, was one of the most senior men in the Foreign and Commonwealth Office. It was arranged that I should report to him personally the following morning. Fontwell wrung my hand as I left, with professional urbanity.

'This is a do-or-die for you, Oliver,' he said.

'You mean it's a perilous assignment?' I asked nervously. With my dear mother in poor health in Sevenoaks, I should not have thought it wise to undertake undue physical risk. Besides, nature has not geared me for high adventure. I am not in the first flush of youth. And my figure, though still admired, is neither lean nor spare.

'You really are a booby,' added Fontwell, almost with affection. 'I was speaking metaphorically. But I do beg you not to foul it up this time. It's your great chance.'

The words inspired me. My little local difficulty would soon be dispelled. I should then be back in the mainstream of promotion. I envisaged myself, in the not too distant future, reigning over some great Embassy. It would be my natural level. With a knighthood of course and possibly even a life peerage. I mentally imagined the authorized biography. 'Mandrake. *The Years of Endurance.*'

Gripping Fontwell's arid paw, which felt a bit like that of a lizard, I almost skipped out into Whitehall.

That evening I met Debbie again. She was a sweet girl. We had seen each other at intervals during my leaves from Washington. For some extraordinary reason, she still had confidence in me.

'Oh, Oliver darling,' she twittered, 'how gorgeous to be with you again.'

'Quite marvellous,' I murmured.

For some reason the poor girl did not bring out the best in me. There was something too insipid about her English-rose beauty. It was satisfactory to know that she still cared about me. But I was now used to gamier meat. How could I forget

5

that voluptuous lady financier in Nashville, Tennessee, where I had been speaking on Britain's economic ills? After a sedate dinner at the Voyagers Club, I escorted Debbie home to her mother's flat in Pelham Crescent but resisted the offer of further entertainment.

'I believe in you, Oliver,' she said simply.

'Thank you, darling.'

'Oh, I know they say you're stuffy and pompous and all that.'

'Who says that?' I replied, somewhat aggrieved.

'But I think you have a remarkable future. As well as an interesting past. You were born under a lucky star.'

'One can only hope so.'

'This new temporary assignment. I hope it's not dangerous.'

'Of course not.'

How laughingly I spoke. If I had only known! I was actually on the threshold of a quite desperate adventure.

Sir Edmund Byfield leaned back and screwed up his shrewd, pale eyes. The tepid London sun might have been disturbing him. Or perhaps he wanted to sharpen his visual impression of me. In spite of his formidable reputation as a linguist, he was actually a man of few words. But he could be impressively taciturn in a dozen languages.

'Tell me about yourself, Mandrake,' he snapped.

It was just the kind of thing I do well. Warming to the well-loved theme, I dwelled modestly on some of my early successes – Polonius in the school Hamlet, President of the Oxford University Food and Wine Society, followed by some years as a debutantes' delight and then my brilliant *coup* in the remote Asian country of Lomsak. I had been instrumental there in tracing the murderer of the Personal Assistant to the British Ambassador.* Since then, as Fontwell had unkindly pointed out, my career had been rather peripatetic. My entry of posts in the Foreign Office list was already awkwardly long.

* See *None of Us Cared for Kate* (1968)

'I gather that you haven't always got on with superiors. And their wives,' commented Byfield grimly.

'Perhaps I need more scope.' I countered. It seemed immodest to suggest that I am a natural leader rather than an acolyte. But I managed to indicate that possibility rather delicately with a determined motion of the chin.

'Well, you don't seem the conventional type,' conceded Byfield.

He was beginning to appreciate my quality. My apologia had clearly impressed this experienced judge of character. I felt emboldened to mention some of the amusing incidents in my more recent career. I can be entertaining enough when I want to, as my dear mother often informs me. Byfield's gnarled countenance eventually creased into a wintry smile. Not for the first time, I realized that my charm had worked the trick. I was in the middle of a complicated anecdote involving a viscountess and a Mexican bishop when I noticed Sir Edmund glancing at a strategically placed grandfather clock. One is far too old a hand to wish to bore senior persons. My antennae warned me to draw deftly to a close.

'Thank you, Mandrake,' he said simply. 'I know you better now.'

That was gratifying news. I suppose I am a bit of an acquired taste.

'I only wish I could sit here all day listening to your – er – reminiscences,' continued the mandarin. 'But I have an appointment at noon with the Secretary of State. You have already convinced me that you are just the man for my project.'

'Thank you,' I murmured gratefully.

'Your curriculum vitae scared me at first,' continued Sir Edmund. 'I will not deny that. But now I see that you are a person of parts.'

His thick glasses sparkled. In a lesser man one might have suspected irony. But officials of Byfield's seniority do not treat public business as a jest.

'I haven't time to go into details now,' he continued. 'But I can brief you for the first part of the assignment. We'll talk again after that. It's all to do with Ruritania. People often talk as if the country were merely the product of a novelist's imagination. But, as you well know, there really is a

7

Ruritania. Just as there really is a Timbuctoo.'

'Albania and Ruritania,' I commented sagely, 'the two unknown countries of eastern Europe.'

'Exactly. We need to build up our links with both. It's absurd not to have diplomatic relations with strategic countries in the middle of Europe. Ruritania of course has changed a bit since Anthony Hope wrote those novels about it. Now it's a People's Socialist Republic and a member of the Warsaw Pact.'

'Have we no diplomatic mission in Strelsau?' I asked brightly. I have always been strong on the capitals of Europe.

'Nothing at all. We broke with them in the late forties over a trade dispute. Until now it has hardly seemed worth reactivating our relations. But Ruritania is becoming steadily more important. So the Foreign and Commonwealth Office is beaming in that direction the piercing rays of its ratiocinatory powers.'

Sir Edmund was being primly facetious. I smiled winningly to show that I had taken the point.

'What do you want me to do?' I asked helpfully.

'It will involve your moving in royal circles.'

My heart sang. My dear mother and aunt have always been keen on the royal family. How thrilled they would be to learn of my promotion up the social ladder. Though by no means a snob, I always feel happier among persons of distinction.

'Or would-be royal circles,' added the Deputy Under-Secretary with a deflating gesture.

'What do you mean?'

'With your knowledge of European royalty and aristocracy, Mandrake, you will no doubt be aware that the ancient family of the Elphbergs ruled Ruritania from the Middle Ages until shortly before the First World War. Of course the People's Republic will have nothing to do with them. But a junior branch of the family live here in England, where they bear the name of Rassendyll.'

'Family name of the Earl of Burlesdon,' I commented snappily.

'Well done, Mandrake. I can see you're well up in the things that matter. Unfortunately Lord Burlesdon can be of little help to us. He suffers from delusions and leads a life of – er – seclusion. There's a streak of fantasy in the whole family.

8

Hence those absurd novels.'

'Can the Rassendylls be of any real importance to Ruritania in this modern age?' I asked. It never does any harm to show that one is up to date and on the ball.

'Certainly they can. They have something very tangible to offer. The man to contact is the effective head of the family, Burlesdon's twin brother, Brigadier Rassendyll. He has an estate in Sussex. A bit of a tartar, I should say. You'll just have to deploy your charm. Tell him some of your – er – amusing stories. A little light badinage might do the trick.'

'What trick?' I asked, feeling quite bewildered. 'Are you asking me to go and interview this Brigadier Rassendyll? If so, why?'

'That, my dear Mandrake,' countered Byfield quite kindly, 'will be explained. But I can't afford to keep the Foreign Secretary waiting. He keeps his famous charm for foreigners, not for me. Why don't you join me for lunch?'

'With pleasure,' I replied warmly. A scrumptious repast at Sir Edmund's expense would be most welcome. I am particularly partial to smoked salmon and a good steak. He might take me to Black's, the aristocratic club in St James's Street to which, as I happened to know, he had at last secured admission.

'I've seen you before in the downstairs room at the Voyagers,' continued the great man. 'Let's meet there at one-fifteen.'

Just my luck, I thought sadly, to be invited to share a scratch meal in the cheap lunch room of one's own club. But at least I should be seen there in the company of one of the most eminent men in the Service. It would do no harm to my standing in the Club. That had never been quite the same since Juanita made that scene in the ladies' annexe.

'I hope you're fond of kedgeree,' said Sir Edmund. 'There's bubble and squeak too.'

'Delicious,' I mumbled.

'I'd like to treat you to a beer. Half a pint?'

'If it's all the same to you,' I riposted, 'I should prefer some of the Club claret.'

My host eyed me warily. It would do him no harm to know

that he was dealing with no spineless worm. There was a point beyond which I could not be bullied. Besides, there are only so many lunches in a lifetime.

We had secured a small table to ourselves. Sir Edmund bent towards me in a conspiratorial whisper.

'I suppose I'd better tell you,' he croaked, 'just what we want you to get out of Brigadier Rassendyll.'

With all the skill to be expected of a senior diplomat of hawk-like intelligence, he explained the requirement only too clearly. It spoiled my meal.

'You're joking,' I gasped.

'Do I look as if I were joking?' snapped Byfield grimly.

'He won't like it at all,' I faltered.

'You can but try.'

'It could be a painful interview.'

'You're an experienced diplomatist, Mandrake. You must have had a few painful interviews in your time.' That was only too true.

'I am far from confident of success.'

'Nothing in this business is going to be easy, Mandrake. That's why we needed a man of spirit. Let's see some of that fire and gusto you showed towards Clementina Baxendale. I have always detested her myself.'

A man of spirit! It was a rousing phrase and by no means an inapt description of my personality. I felt better after that. The Club claret too had produced a gently warming effect.

'I'll have a go then,' I murmured weakly.

'Thank you, Oliver. I knew you wouldn't let me down. In fact, I mentioned to the Foreign Secretary only just now that we had a good man on the job.'

'The Foreign Secretary! Is he personally involved?'

'Certainly. He's deeply into Ruritania these days. He badly needs a foreign policy success to keep the Party happy.'

'Is the country all that important?'

'It's moving up fast. Their natural gas deposits are significant. So is their chrome. And of course their geographical position has become a key one, with all this sensitivity over troop movements. You know how delicate the European balance is today. Ministers are deeply concerned. They feel that our foreign policy can no longer afford to neglect the Strelsau dimension.'

10

The Strelsau dimension! It was an arresting phrase. And I was to be the standard bearer of this important new shift of policy. I flushed with pleasure at the prospect of a glittering future. It was ever thus in our island story. Britain has always been able to call in the hour of need on the lone hero. Gordon of Khartoum. Scott of the Antarctic. Mandrake of Strelsau.

'Let's have coffee in the morning room,' suggested Sir Edmund. 'It's included in the price of the lunch.'

'Can this be the right place?' I asked the Foreign Office driver.

'Looks a rum spot to me,' came the comforting reply.

The great gates and the long drive were grand enough. But Brigadier Rassendyll's Sussex estate, if indeed it was, seemed strangely forbidding. The overgrown bushes and tangled grass appeared curiously out of place in one of the trimmest of the home counties. Nor was the house itself more welcoming, when we eventually reached it. Built in the uncompromising style of nineteenth-century Gothic, its curly pinnacles could have come straight out of a horror story set in central Europe. Clearly the Rassendylls were one of those idiosyncratic families who create their own ethos. For the first time I sensed the heady and vaguely sinister atmosphere attached to the mysterious country of Ruritania. It was hard to believe that, all around us, prosperous stockbrokers would shortly be returning from the City for their evening whiskies.

I alighted doubtfully. There seemed no sign of life in the gloomy mansion.

'See you later, guv,' said the driver, beginning to turn his car.

'Wait for me here please,' I instructed.

'Can't do that, I'm afraid. Got to pick up one of your colleagues at Gatwick airport. But he only wants to go to Three Bridges. I'll be back in an hour and a half or less. If the plane's on time.'

'But you're booked for me. It's a mission of national importance.'

'Sorry, Sir. I can only go by my time-sheet. It says you have to double up.'

How like the Foreign Office to jeopardize my task at the outset with a niggling economy of this type. I waved to my

11

driver with a touch of hauteur as he screeched off down the dusty gravel towards the distant main road. Then I rang the bell of the main door. It clanked ominously. I felt very much alone. Inwardly I cursed smooth-talking Sir Edmund who had landed me in this painful predicament.

Nobody answered the bell. The house seemed quite deserted. With my heart beating nervously, I leaned against the door and turned the handle. It opened with surprising ease. As I stepped across the threshold into a small lobby and then the main hall, some instinct told me to be more than usually careful. As a professional diplomat of some seniority and experience, I have developed my antennae over the years. Extrasensory perception seldom lets me down.

The hall was baronial in style. Guns and stags' antlers decorated the walls. The place was clearly a bit of a white elephant. I crossed into a small study which bore signs of recent activity. It contained a useful desk and a strong-looking safe with a tough combination-lock. Was it here that I should find what I had come to seek? It seemed more than possible. Outright burglary was a tempting option. But I lack the necessary technical skill. Besides, the Foreign Office would be furious. My mission was to attain the prize through charm and persuasive skill. That was why they had selected me.

It would do no harm, I thought, to open the desk drawer. By some extraordinary chance, it might contain something of relevance to my mission. In any case, I am curious by nature and never miss a chance to pry. The desk was a low one and I felt obliged to bend. It was therefore not in the small of the back but somewhat lower in the body that I suddenly felt the unwelcome pressure of cold metal. Naturally I recoiled in horror, as a voice hissed in my ear.

'Take it easy, Nightshade. You don't want a bullet up the back-side.'

Five minutes later, as we sat in huge oak chairs, I had an opportunity to inspect more conveniently the masterful, weather-beaten countenance of Brigadier the Honourable Rudolph Rassendyll, M.C. It was a face that might have been painted by Rembrandt with a dash of Franz Hals. The face of

12

a freebooter or soldier of fortune rather than a member of one of the great European families. But a face born to command all right. There was no mistaking the message in that arrogant nose, cold blue eyes and flaming red hair. I was reminded of the bloodstained origins of the mediaeval Elphbergs who treated Ruritania as a feudal fief for centuries. Every schoolboy knows of the Defenestration of Strelsau, one of the less unspeakable atrocities ascribed to Henry the Lion, the most renowned leader of the House of Elphberg. The Brigadier looked as if defenestration would come quite easily as part of the day's work. Thank Heaven we were on the ground floor. That pistol point had left me sore enough as it was.

'Forgive me for being a bit rough,' said the Brigadier disarmingly 'but I can't afford to take chances. One has enemies.'

'Enemies? In peaceful England.'

'Certainly. For all practical purposes, I now represent the royal family of Ruritania in the West. I am by no means without support in the country itself. So I pose a constant threat to the Government in Strelsau. They'd be delighted to get rid of me.'

'Would they really harm you?'

'It cannot be ruled out, Hemlock. That's why I leave the door deliberately open. To ensnare my opponents. I almost peppered you just now. You made an awfully tempting target. From the rear you might well have been a plump Marxist.'

'But surely you were expecting me? I thought the Foreign Office had telephoned.'

'I remembered just in time. They told me a Mr Valentine Mortmain would call.'

'The name,' I said coolly, 'is Mandrake. Oliver Mandrake.'

'Of course. Had a dentist of that name once. Bit him as a boy.'

The Brigadier was clearly out to emphasize the difference in our social positions. His manner was far from sympathetic. But I am by no means unused to coping with tough nuts. I favoured him with one of my level stares.

'Hope you're enjoying the tipple,' snapped the Brigadier.

'It has a taste all its own.'

'Ruritanian cherry brandy. It's got a kick like a mule.'

13

I felt as if I'd swallowed fire-water. But I wasn't going to give this odious bully the satisfaction of seeing me flinch.

'So the Foreign Office is becoming interested in Ruritania,' continued Rassendyll unkindly. 'At least I can introduce you to the cuisine. Some people say it's rather highly flavoured. But of course my family are used to that. If you'll stay for dinner, my daughter produces a powerful peppered pork stew. It's the national weapon.'

My throat was burning, my eyes streaming.

'Water please,' I gasped at last.

'I thought you might want some,' said my host, more kindly. 'You should have asked before.'

Round one to Rassendyll. But we Mandrakes have hidden resilience.

'And now to business,' continued the veteran. 'What on earth do the Foreign Office want of me?'

The moment of truth had arrived. I felt a sinking feeling. That ass Byfield had placed me in a ludicrous situation.

'They are very conscious of the strategic and economic importance of your country,' I replied evasively.

'It's not my country,' roared the Brigadier. 'I'm as British as you are. Went to Harrow and Brasenose. Just take a natural interest in poor benighted Ruritania, that's all.'

'Quite, quite,' I murmured soothingly. He was the sort of senior officer who would once have had rebellious sepoys blown from cannons. 'Well, Ruritania is on the map now. The Strelsau dimension, you know.'

Rassendyll threw back his leonine head and roared dramatically.

'That's rich,' he shouted, 'damned rich. At last Her Majesty's Government takes an interest in Ruritania. About eighty years too late. If they'd bothered to lift a finger, they could have kept the Elphbergs on the throne when old Queen Flavia died. But they preferred to keep in with the bloody Hapsburgs who were always suspicious of our lot. Britain saw the Hapsburgs as a bulwark against the Hohenzollerns in Prussia. The old diplomacy was a series of Chinese boxes, each within the other. We were a pawn in the great game. And what good did it do? They were all smashed to smithereens – Hapsburgs, Hohenzollerns, Elphbergs, the whole shooting match. I'm still alive though.'

14

He glared moodily through the uncleaned window onto the uncut lawn.

'Is that Queen Flavia's picture?' I enquired mildly.

'Damned fine woman, isn't she?'

'Remarkable.' The face in the royal portrait might have launched a thousand ships. But only with evacuees. It had the remnants of great beauty, mingled with a most unpleasing arrogance.

'Only crowned head in Europe with the guts to stand up to Queen Victoria,' croaked the Brigadier.

'Was she the last ruling Elphberg?' I asked.

'She was the last to rule in Strelsau. So far. But the royal house have never abandoned their claims. They will come back.'

'How interesting,' I replied mildly. 'Well, that's just what I wanted to talk about.'

That is the great advantage of being a trained diplomat. One acquires an instinctive feel for the right moment to launch a negotiating gambit. It has often stood me in good stead.

'You mean you're restoring the Elphbergs?'

'Well, not exactly. Not just at the moment. Britain's power in Europe has somewhat shrunk since the days of Queen Flavia. But we do want to resume diplomatic relations with Ruritania. It's high time we reopened our Embassy in Strelsau. Strictly for your own information, Brigadier, a British team will shortly be leaving for Strelsau to start negotiations with the Government there over outstanding problems.'

'And you want me to lead the team?' The old buccaneer's face glowed at the thought.

'Well, not exactly. But you could help.'

'This is heady news, Nightshade. Of course you'll have to press for satisfaction. The royal estates were confiscated. I've got all the details. Have another snorter.'

'No, thank you. As you indicate, Brigadier, our negotiators will need all the support they can get. Something will have to be done, for example, about the Elphberg emeralds. You know about them of course?'

'Know about them! My dear man, I have frequently explored the possibility of restoring them forcibly to their rightful ownership. But the security arrangements in the British Museum are abominably thorough. It is a perfect scandal that they were not handed to me when they were first brought to Britain after the Second World War.'

'It all seems a long time ago.'

'Not to me, Nightshade. It was the one chance to get them back for our family. They're magnificent gems, perhaps the finest emeralds in Europe. Queen Flavia is wearing them in that portrait. When the so-called Republic came, they were nationalized and kept in the Strelsau Museum. Then the Nazis took them away to Germany and the British army got hold of them after the War. I was their rightful custodian in Britain. But the new Government in Strelsau claimed them as a national treasure. In its usual spineless way, our Government compromised by just sticking them in the British Museum. Yes, I do know about the Elphberg emeralds.'

'Strelsau is greatly interested in them. It's funny how keen these modern communist governments are on the old royal mementos of their countries. National pride, I suppose. The Russians have restored the czarist churches in the Kremlin.'

'They're not getting the Elphberg emeralds. Over my dead body.'

'Oh come, Brigadier. One must live in the real world. A decision has already been taken.'

'What decision?'

'The British Government has no legal right to keep the emeralds. They are part of the Ruritanian crown jewels. If we re-establish diplomatic relations with Ruritania, we inevitably recognize the existence of the modern Ruritanian State. We are therefore obliged in law to hand the emeralds over to the legally constituted Government in Strelsau.'

'I don't accept that. The jewels belong to the House of Elphberg. They should be passed to me.'

'But you don't claim to be King of Ruritania?'

'No. There are still real Elphbergs living privately in Ruritania. But I represent their interests here.'

'Surely you must see, my dear Brigadier, that there is no hope of our doing a diplomatic deal with the people in Strelsau unless we satisfy them over the emeralds. It's a point of national pride. We shall return them to Ruritania without fuss. They belong there anyway. If you've got to give way in the long run, it's best to make a generous gesture at the outset.

16

It will be a valuable concession for our negotiators to be able to offer.'

'Appeasement,' shouted the man of war, his old gargoyle of a face beginning to deepen to a dark purple colour. He cast a malevolent glance towards the corner where a serviceable horse-whip was carelessly lying. It was a situation that needed defusing. My experienced antennae signalled to me accordingly.

'I'm sorry you should feel that,' I said calmly. 'Handled with care, the position could have been exploited to the great advantage of the Elphbergs and the Rassendylls.'

'How?'

'You too have an interest in coming to terms with the present Government of Ruritania. They are much more reasonable these days. They might be willing to compensate you for the loss of family estates and property. And who knows? A movement might even develop towards the restoration of royal privileges.'

Privately, I did not consider this at all likely. But I am a wily negotiator and the brute had to be handled.

'With this in mind,' I continued smoothly, 'it will be desirable for you to be associated with the return to Strelsau of the Elphberg emeralds.'

'That's easy,' snapped the Brigadier. 'The British Museum can give them to me. And I'll – er – deal with the matter.'

'No, I'm afraid there must be a direct transfer.'

'Then how can I be linked with it?'

'There is a way,' I replied with quiet aplomb. Fatuous though the Foreign Office proposal seemed to me, it had to be presented with dignity and assurance. 'You could add to the emeralds, for presentation in Strelsau, something which is in your own keeping. That would convince the Ruritanian authorities of your good-will.'

'What do you mean, Mortmain?'

'The Rassendyll ruby,' I said simply.

I have seldom seen a man so angry. The Brigadier fairly hopped around the room, as if in intense pain, his face contorted with rage.

'The Rassendyll ruby!' he shrieked. 'You're a perfect bloody nincompoop.'

'It was a Foreign Office idea,' I added limply.

'Are you not aware, man, that the Rassendyll ruby has been in our family in England since the eighteenth century? We're descended from an Elphberg who sowed his wild oats in England before going home to Ruritania to become King. He gave the ruby to my distinguished ancestress as payment for services rendered. Good, honest, straightforward services too. We're the English bastards descended from a tart. They gave us the Burlesdon title in a vain attempt to make us respectable.'

'The Ruritanian Government would love to get hold of the Rassendyll ruby, as well as the Elphberg emeralds.'

'I'll bet they would. But they won't.'

'Is that your considered reply?'

'It certainly is. Anyone who tries to deprive me of the Rassendyll ruby will get a very nasty surprise. You're a complete damned fool. I should have spotted that earlier. Didn't you know that I'm extremely unsympathetic to the People's Republic of Ruritania?'

'Oh come, Brigadier. We are pursuing *détente* policies in Europe now.'

'I'm not, Nightshade. I'm an old-fashioned royalist. Call me a fascist, if you like. I know perfectly well that Strelsau will do nothing for me. And I'm doing nothing for them. That is final.'

He looked awfully like a bull about to charge. Instinct told me that the moment had come to make a dignified departure.

'Then I won't detain you longer,' I said, rising with professional urbanity.

'You won't stay for some of Flavia's peppered pork soup?'

'No, thank you,' I almost shrieked.

The Brigadier accompanied me to the front door across the gloomy hall. He flung it open with an expansive gesture.

'Take a tip from me, Hemlock,' he said nastily. 'Keep right away from Ruritania. It's too complicated for you.'

'The name's Mandrake,' I snapped. 'As you know perfectly well. I've enjoyed meeting you, Brigadier. It has helped me to understand one thing. What the Ruritanian people had to put up with before the Revolution.'

It was an effective exit line. But it caused my host to slam the door with a bang. I found myself alone in the drive. I looked around expectantly for the Foreign Office limousine. It had been an exhausting interview and I looked forward to a

18

quiet drive back to London. But no car was to be seen. The wretched driver must still be on the way back from the airport.

Dusk was beginning to fall across the Park. I did not care for the prospect of just standing in front of the house. The half-crazed Brigadier might well take a pot shot at me from an upper window. It would be best to follow a path which looked like a short cut through the shrubbery to the lodge at the main gate. I could join my car there.

It was not one of my better ideas. After a few minutes' walk, I heard the howling of the dogs.

'Poor Mr Mandrake,' said Flavia Rassendyll. 'Were you a tiny bit afraid?'

I gave her one of my long, hard stares. They can be remarkably effective with presumptuous junior persons. The girl's colour freshened. With that reddish hair, she blushed easily.

'I am grateful for your help.' I replied urbanely. 'But your father should have warned me.'

The young man Henry snorted. In his case the Rassendyll nose, as unmistakable as the Hapsburg lip, was unattractively elongated.

'Dad probably assumed you could handle dogs,' he replied. 'All our friends can.'

I eyed him in frigid silence. He stood for all I most dislike – early rising, cold country houses, savage animals, mud on one's best suede shoes, horse-play in the billiard room.

'Dogs have always been a thing in our family,' commented Flavia brightly. 'The mediaeval Elphbergs had quite a name for it. Their enemies accused them of being werewolves in disguise. You know, people who change at night into wolves.'

It seemed far from impossible. I could just imagine Henry and his carnivorous father loping through the park by moonlight.

'I am looking for the Foreign Office car,' I said crisply.

'It will be there by the main gate. You can just see the roof of the lodge. You must be the man that Daddy was expecting.'

'Yes.'

'Did you have a nice chat?'

19

'We did our business.'

'He's sweet, isn't he?' continued Flavia. 'Daddy, I mean.'

'Not really.'

'You must get to know him better, Mr Mandrake. Why not come back to the house for dinner? I'm cooking peppered pork goulash.'

'No, thank you,' I replied with a shudder.

'Well, at least let me offer you a cup of tea. After your ordeal. I cook up at the house. But I actually live in the lodge when I'm down here. It's my own place. I have a flat in town too, of course.'

The girl spoke lightly but there was a stimulating hint of invitation in her voice.

'I can't make it,' said Henry. 'Got to take the dogs home.'

'Then I shall have to entertain poor Mr Mandrake,' said Flavia. 'He still looks quite shaky.'

I was in fact shaking with pleasurable anticipation. With my usual delicate sensitivity, I had quickly spotted that this aristocratic and wilful girl was eager for a chance to be alone with me. Once again my fatal charm had found a victim. I have often wondered why I am attractive to women. I am neither slim nor conventionally handsome. But the years have given me a certain dignified urbanity which has sometimes proved irresistible. In the circumstances there seems little point in getting married. Some people think me selfish but I have to fulfil my destiny.

'Perhaps I should rest for a little,' I agreed, with one of my saucy twinkles.

'Have another biscuit, Mr Mandrake?'

'Thank you. I can never refuse. It's one of my weaknesses.'

'So I notice, Mr Mandrake.'

'Do call me Oliver.'

It was a cosy scene. Flavia had promisingly drawn the curtains, though this did not seem strictly necessary, since it was not yet completely dark. We were sitting together on a comfortable sofa in her trim living-room. The cottage was tiny but in perfect order, unlike the main house. Upstairs there would be a small bedroom. Flavia was no mean organizer.

20

'What exactly are you doing, Oliver?'

I was in fact running my hand gently down the girl's right thigh. It felt pleasantly warm through the material. Considerable experience has taught me that it is best to begin the proceedings in an almost absent-minded manner. The girl can then pretend that she did not notice what was happening until it was too late. In this field, as in diplomacy, it is important to help the partner to save face. I am all for finesse. The modern permissive method of just flinging off one's clothes is like tucking into a steak without sherry and soup first. Relations between men and women should start as a stately gavotte, even if they culminate in a scherzo. I could lecture rather well on the subject to one of those courses for new entrants to the Diplomatic Service.

'You are lovely, Flavia,' I murmured. My hand was motionless now, but I had not removed it.

The girl smiled enigmatically. It was the mocking, mysterious glance of the Mona Lisa. I felt deeply moved. Trumpets were sounding in the brain. But I must act with my usual circumspection. I was doing this for the nation. A successful love affair with Flavia would offer the best possible chance of securing the Rassendyll ruby. How pleased Sir Edmund would be, if he could see us now. It is a hard life in the British Diplomatic Service. But just occasionally it is still possible to mix business with pleasure.

'A penny for your thoughts, Oliver.'

'I was thinking what a charming view there must be from the top floor. Through the trees.'

'Come and see.'

Rising hastily, I followed the girl up the narrow staircase. Old-fashioned etiquette books say that gentlemen should precede ladies up ladders. But it is more fun the other way round. The prospect of Flavia's swelling curves was enough to divert anyone's attention from foreign policy considerations.

'What a beautiful bed,' I commented breathlessly.

'Yes, isn't it? It came originally from the Castle of Zenda and has long historical connections. A gift from my namesake, Queen Flavia. Several generations of my family have died in it. But it's considered very unlucky to make love in the Zenda bed. That's why it's always used by the eldest virgin in the family.'

Was she teasing me? There was something devilish about that red hair and mocking smile. But I am not easily fooled. I looked down pointedly at a fleecy, sheepskin rug on the floor. It was a magic moment.

It is difficult to put your hand absent-mindedly on a girl's thigh when you are both standing up. The gesture becomes too obvious. Fortunately my technique caters for every situation. With a kindly, avuncular movement I laid my hand on Flavia's shoulder and then let it slip down towards the prominent bosom.

'You're a silly fellow, Oliver. I thought you were a high-powered diplomat. But you're just like the others.'

'I'm not like the others at all. I'm splendid and special.'

Prove it, said the expression on her face. Suddenly my long experience gave me an insight into what she really wanted. This girl needed to be overcome by an elemental force of nature, to be swept off her feet by a wave of the ocean. It was a role which suited me quite well. Upper-class girls often respond to rough treatment. Something of my new determination must have showed upon my face. Flavia gasped.

'Another cup of tea?' she murmured faintly, 'Or a little sherry?'

'This is no time for sherry,' I snapped grimly, pushing the girl firmly backwards towards the Zenda bed. There is a caveman side to my nature which needs expression every now and then. It is a mistake to bottle up one's emotions. Psychiatrists are agreed about that.

'Please, Oliver. Do be sensible. Can't we just talk?'

'Too late for talk,' I snapped. 'You have a rendezvous with reality.'

'Mercy' she shrieked, quite convincingly, 'Have mercy!'

It was a most stimulating situation. With a savage growl, I seized Flavia and forced her downwards onto the Zenda bed. Now I was covering her appetising little face with kisses. Were the sounds beneath me grunts of despair or squeals of pleasure? It was too late to care. I had heard church-bells beyond the stars.

I sudden surge of pain in my lower back brought me to my senses. With a howl of agony, I leaped off the bed.

'You little minx,' I yelled.

Flavia rose coolly.

'I only dug in my nails,' she explained. 'I thought you might like it.'

'You're a horrible sadist, Flavia. Am I bleeding?'

'Not profusely.'

I gave the girl one of my most impressive stares. Indignation was in it, and righteous anger, and profound sadness.

'You look so funny, Oliver. Like a greedy schoolboy who finds the sweetshop shut.'

Her mockery drove me to fury. I flung myself upon the impertinent wench. But the result was unexpected. Instead of feeling her yield before me, I suddenly found myself rising in the air and then sailing through it. In a second I was lying on the floor at the other end of the room, with the sensation of having broken every bone in my body.

'My spine has snapped,' I groaned. 'Get an ambulance.'

'Nonsense, you silly plump booby. I know how to throw a man. You're only a tiny bit bruised.'

'You're a fiend, Flavia.'

'Not quite that. Just a girl who has to look after herself. Daddy made us learn.'

'I'm a broken man.'

'It will be a useful lesson to you, Oliver. To treat the House of Elphberg with respect.'

She helped the bewildered driver to put me gingerly into the car. Happy laughter rang from the turreted lodge as we drove away. I sincerely hoped that I would have no more dealings with the old royal house of Ruritania. But hopes are not always gratified.

'I hear you had trouble with the Rassendylls,' said Sir Edmund Byfield calmly.

My heart sank. Perhaps the lodge had been bugged and the whole painful scene was now recorded on tape in the Foreign Office. If so, there would be unseemly laughter at my expense. I prefer to make the jokes myself.

'Brigadier Rudy was telling them about it in the bar at Black's last night,' explained Sir Edmund. 'Claims to have set the dogs on you. Or so my cronies inform me. He didn't seem at all keen on handing over the Rassendyll ruby.'

'He did indeed reply in the negative,' I answered with simple dignity.

'I thought he would,' said Byfield calmly.

'Well, why did you make me go and ask for it?' I enquired, somewhat nettled.

'It was just worth trying. But now you can relax, my dear Oliver. You won't meet the terrible Rassendylls here in the Voyagers. It's sausages and mash today for the quick lunch.'

Was Byfield just using me? I eyed him with suspicion.

'What happens now?' I asked cautiously.

'We go forward as planned,' said the dynamic Sir Edmund. He was in his element now, scheming for Britain. 'Clearly the Rassendyll ruby is not available. But we can still use the Elphberg emeralds as a valuable bargaining counter in the negotiations with Ruritania. The problem is to get them to Strelsau at exactly the right time. Our negotiators will need to produce them at the best possible psychological moment. Like a rabbit out of a hat.'

'Surely that's only a technical difficulty.'

'Not entirely. We cannot risk the emeralds falling into the hands of the Ruritanians except as part of an agreed deal. Otherwise we lose all the advantage. Remember that the Government in Strelsau claims a legal right to the jewels. So if they can get hold of them, they will just keep them. The Foreign Office in London would be left looking pretty silly. It's not a posture we enjoy.'

'You could use the diplomatic bag.'

'Out of the question. We have no diplomatic mission in Strelsau. As you know.'

His glance was a little sharp. The man's computer mind was programmed to take account of every detail. It was no moment to relax. Perhaps on this occasion I had better avoid the Club claret.

'Why shouldn't our negotiating team take the emeralds out with them to Strelsau?' I suggested. 'At this delicate stage of our relations, the Ruritanians would surely not dare to steal the jewels from them.'

'That's a better idea, Oliver. But it won't work. Our team is being led by Lord Pargiter. He's very able but a bit of a prima donna, you know. Works straight to the Foreign Secretary. Pargiter insists that he should not be burdened with responsibility for the emerald until the moment has actually arrived to hand them over.'

'Then they must be taken secretly to Strelsau by a special courier.'

'Exactly, Oliver. You've hit the nail on the head.'

'Perhaps a couple of young fellows from the Outward Bag room.'

'Outward Bag room!' Byfield almost shrieked, quite losing his impressive calm. 'But the emeralds are beyond price. They should really be escorted by a battalion of troops. Since the Ruritanians would never allow that, the only hope lies in complete secrecy and absolute discretion. The courier must be a person of the highest calibre, capable of dealing with any possible emergency.'

'Quite so,' I murmured politely. That was his problem, not mine. It was a relief to hear that the negotiators would not have to bother with the custody of the wretched emeralds.

'I suppose I shall be number two on Lord Pargiter's team,' I continued hopefully. It was a dazzling prospect. Pargiter would soon be utterly dependent on my advice. I should play a key role in these vital negotiations. Accelerated promotion would be the inevitable result.

'Not exactly,' replied Byfield cautiously. 'That slot has already been filled.'

'Anyone I know?'

'Trevor Flask.'

'But I can't possibly work under him. He's a contemporary of mine.'

Flask had always been one of my least favourite colleagues. Aggressively proud of his humble origins, he liked to think of himself as one of the rising stars of the new diplomacy with its interest in trade and horrid technological innovations. I have never concealed my own preference for the older school of diplomacy with its greater emphasis on breeding, style and the niceties of gracious living. Mandrake and Flask, we were like chalk and cheese.

'I know that Flask is your contemporary,' said Byfield with a mollifying gesture. 'You won't be working as part of his team.'

'What shall I be doing then?'

Sir Edmund had the grace to look a little abashed.

25

'You will be the special courier,' he said.

The exterior of the Foreign Office was being expensively cleaned. Streams of water poured down the windows of Byfield's prestigiously large room. It seemed as if we were beneath the surface of the sea. But he appeared quite oblivious of the process.

'It's not a job for a Counsellor,' I protested yet again. He had felt obliged to take me back to the Office after our modest lunch. 'It's a trained security officer you need.'

'That's where I must disagree with you, my dear Oliver. The job is far too delicate for that. It's not a question of simply guarding the emeralds by force. The task is to conceal their whereabouts in Ruritania and then to produce them for Lord Pargiter at exactly the right moment. Only an experienced diplomatist would be competent to take the necessary decisions. You are just the right man.'

'Why don't you swap me with Trevor Flask? I will advise Lord Pargiter. He can bring the jewels.'

'I'm afraid Personnel Department would not agree to that. Flask has a brilliant record. He was a superb head of Central European Department. Pargiter has picked him specially.'

The implication was obvious. Flask, a graduate in chemistry from an obscure northern university, was considered to be in an intellectual league much superior to my own. It was a deeply galling thought.

'I suppose that just anyone can be the courier,' I commented nastily.

'Now, don't be silly, Oliver. You have a highly responsible job too. It's a question of horses for courses. Let me show you something that will cheer you up.'

The Deputy Under Secretary rose and locked the door. Then he crossed to a concealed wall safe which he opened with his habitual efficiency. With a dramatic gesture, he took out a small case which he placed on his imposing desk. He beckoned me to him. Then he pressed a spring and the case flew open. I found myself staring at the crown jewels of Ruritania.

'Superb!' I gasped.

26

'Aren't they gorgeous? Worth a king's ransom. The Director of the British Museum brought them himself this morning.'

The Elphberg emeralds nestled coyly on dark velvet. They were large and green and marvellously brilliant. Their sparkle filled the gloomy room. I felt dazzled and a little humble.

'Men have died for these,' continued Byfield. I thought this a shade tactless of him.

'Not any more, I hope,' I said.

'Don't be nervous, Oliver. Every precaution will be taken. To begin with, we've made you a perfect hiding-place for the gems.'

He showed it to me. It certainly didn't look like a jewel box. But there would just be space enough inside.

'Very ingenious,' I commented. 'But wouldn't they be more secure in a small travelling safe?'

'Certainly not. Everything can be opened these days. The best security is to hide the emeralds somewhere totally unexpected. Nobody will ever look there.'

'I can only hope you're right.'

'We will supply a death pill. You can use it if you're captured and tortured.'

'Tortured!' I shrieked. 'You've chosen quite the wrong man, Sir Edmund. My tolerance of pain is unusually low. My dentist will supply a certificate.'

'Keep calm, Oliver. People will hear you in the corridor. I was joking of course. You're a diplomat, not a secret agent. It's all quite simple. Flask will give you detailed instructions.'

I gave him an icy stare. It really was too bad. First torture and death were mentioned. Now I was sent to take orders from the unspeakable Flask, a man who probably drank Algerian wine and wore synthetic shirts.

'I am not junior to Flask,' I pointed out again.

'Now don't be touchy, Oliver. This is no moment for sterile wrangles over protocol. Flask knows the whole plan. He will fill you in. But I'll see you on the night before you leave. That's when you take delivery of the emeralds. I shall need a receipt.'

'I'll take the death pill then too. Preferably in the form of peppermint pastilles.'

'Well done, Oliver. I'm glad you haven't lost your sense of

humour. It could come in useful. But, joking apart, do take care of yourself. There could be more to this than meets the eye. Britain is relying on you. To get the emeralds through to Strelsau.'

The sight of Trevor Flask somewhat restored my aplomb. In his readymade suit and screwed-up tie, he cut a poor figure beside my own. How glad I was to be wearing my best new worsted suit of delicate herringbone pattern, made for me by Campbell and Custerman of Savile Row. I glanced pointedly at Trevor's scruffy brogues and then at my own well polished black shoes from a little place in Jermyn Street. But he did not appear to notice my ploy. There could be no doubt which of us was better equipped to represent the country one day in a major European capital. I at least looked the part.

'You've put on weight, Oliver,' said Flask cheerfully. 'Must have been at the flesh-pots. I should have written to thank you for your kind letter. When I got my gong.'

He had recently been awarded the C.M.G., somewhat to my chagrin. It was typical of this devotee of equality that he should think it necessary to remind me of this decoration. I smiled wanly.

'I'm very keen on this Ruritania project,' continued Trevor, with that irritating show of enthusiasm which had won him such favour among the upper echelons of the Foreign Office. 'The economic background is so fascinating. I've been studying the statistics for chrome exports. And their hydro-electric potential is enormous.'

'What do I do?'

'You have a key role, Oliver. You produce the emeralds when we need them.'

'I know that. But what do I do until then?'

'A good question,' replied Trevor, with a patronising smile. 'But it's all arranged. You will visit Ruritania as a tourist. It's a perfect cover plan. You had rather a trying time in Washington. Now you need a holiday. Everyone knows that you're madly keen on culture. The mediaeval castles of Ruritania are famous. You will travel out by train. You don't want to be burdened with a car. We have arranged for you to stay at the

28

Zenda Palace Hotel. It's most convenient. Ten miles from the frontier and forty from Strelsau. It will give the game away if you stick too close to us at first.'

'Is it a comfortable hotel?'

'Really, Oliver, you're priceless. It's an old, picturesque place. There must be bathrooms.'

'And where will you be, Trevor?'

'In the Strelsau Hilton. Opened last year.'

'All modern conveniences, no doubt.'

'I hope you're going to be a sport about this, Oliver. You just stay put. Take plenty to read. When we need the emeralds, we'll send you a message inviting you to lunch in Strelsau. A quite natural comradely gesture.'

'Thank you, comrade.'

'There's no need to glower at me, Oliver. I didn't cast the parts in this charade. Some of us have to do the – er – field work.'

'If it comes to field work, Trevor, your wardrobe is more suitable for it than mine.'

'That was unkind, Oliver. I do hope you're not becoming twisted and bitter. We have to work together.'

'It will be an experience to work with you, Trevor. In the people's paradise of Ruritania. You must tell me more about the people.'

'I come from the people, Oliver. I'm not ashamed of that. I'm glad I didn't go to some struggling minor public school, full of struggling minor people. I concentrate on essentials. And I don't care about the difference between Manet and Monet or Gaddi and Daddi. So don't try to be snooty with me. It won't work.'

I was glad to have provoked him. It made him look more vulnerable. Poor little chap, trying to make his own way in the world. I gave him a benign smile.

'My dear Trevor,' I said with my usual old-world urbanity, 'we shall make an excellent team. You with your knowledge of chrome and chemistry. I with my flair for the beautiful and the baroque. Where you end, I begin.'

'Yes,' snapped Flask. 'And where I begin, you end.'

29

'A holiday,' said my dear mother. 'What fun! Margot and I can come with you.'

'That would have been delightful,' I replied hastily. 'But a little too strenuous for you both, I fear. It will be a kind of walking tour.'

'That doesn't sound like you, Oliver,' commented my aunt. 'You were always a lazy boy.'

'Is Ruritania quite safe?' asked Mother. 'I thought it was a communist country.'

'We're on fairly good terms with them these days.'

'It all seems peculiar to me,' continued my aunt. 'You've been having a holiday in England. You should be going to another diplomatic post. Perhaps they don't want you.'

'Nonsense, Margot. Oliver is very highly thought of by the Foreign Office. I met a retired ambassador at the Archdeacon's garden party. He said that Oliver had quite a reputation.'

'It must be a secret mission.'

'I wish you wouldn't say that, Auntie. Careless talk costs lives.'

'I thought it was something important,' said my aunt triumphantly.

'Just you keep quiet, Margot. Oliver knows what he's doing. He's a big boy now.'

They beamed at me benevolently. One needs to be a hero to somebody.

'Ruritania,' exclaimed Debbie with a slightly irritating giggle. 'I'll come with you.'

'That would have been delightful. But a little too strenuous, I fear. It will be a kind of walking tour.'

'But I love walking.'

'There could be complications.'

'Nothing dangerous, I hope? You're precious to me.'

'Thank you.'

'I don't know why. You're a bit of an old idiot. But you do make a nice, cuddly teddy bear.'

'I feel flattered.'

'We could make it permanent, if you like.'

My extrasensory perception told me that we were on the edge of a pitfall. This artful girl was trying to lure me into marriage. That is the snag about being an eligible bachelor.

'We'll talk about it later,' I said. 'On my return. If I return.'

'If you return!' she wailed. 'Oh, Oliver, it's just as I feared. This is some mad, quixotic adventure. Why did you volunteer?'

'I have to do it, darling. For the sake of honour. And the free world.'

There was a glint in the girl's eye. Apprehension had excited her. I might have been a racing driver. Fortunately her family were in the country. We had the top floor of Pelham Crescent to ourselves. I felt rather mouldy in the morning.

'This is the frontier,' said the old lady. 'There will be a long wait.'

It was a spine-chilling moment. Across there, in the dark woods, Ruritania began. In the nineteenth century the route lay through Dresden. But now it was more convenient to travel via Vienna and Budapest and then north-east to this long forgotten corner of eastern Europe. Here Ruritania nestled in the mountains between Czechoslovakia, Romania and the Soviet Union. A presentiment of danger struck me as I looked out at the border guards on the stark platform. I had been crazy to let myself in for such a ridiculous project. And I had no diplomatic protection either. If caught with my precious freight, I should be at the mercy of these unknown people.

'Have you anything to declare?' asked the old lady. 'They will want to know.'

We had struck up an acquaintance in the train leaving Vienna. Guessing my nationality, she had addressed me in English. She was the widow of a Ruritanian doctor and had been visiting a niece in Paris. Our talk had been most friendly and I had given her a modified version of my holiday plans.

'You will love Zenda, Mr Mandrake,' she had said. 'It's the old royal capital of our country. The Castle is genuinely mediaeval. It even has a moat and a drawbridge. It's an ancient stronghold of the House of Elphberg.'

I shuddered.

31

'Will I be staying there?'

'Not exactly. Connected with the Castle is the baroque palace built in the eighteenth century. It is on the town side of the moat and much more comfortable. The modern hotel is in the palace, not the Castle.'

That sounded more promising. I am all for picturesque squalor. But not for myself.

Now the immigration and customs officials had entered our compartment. Were they really giving me grim and suspicious looks or was it just my overwrought imagination?

'They ask you,' said the old lady kindly, 'whether you have anything to declare. Currency. Perfume. Jewellery.'

It was the point of no return. I felt an intense urge to glance up at the rack where one of my suitcases contained the crown jewels of Ruritania. But I managed to resist the temptation. That is the advantage of being a trained diplomat. It does enable one to confront such situations with urbane sang-froid.

'Please tell them,' I replied with massive calm, 'that I have nothing to declare.'

They examined my passport, stamped my visa and passed on. Eventually the train started to move again. We were entering the deep forests of Ruritania.

'Are you all right, Mr Mandrake?' asked the old lady, bending forward anxiously. 'You have turned rather pale.'

Something was wrong. I could feel it in my bones. I turned and locked with a huge key the door of my capacious bedroom in the Zenda Palace Hotel. Then I drew the strong iron bolts at the top and bottom of the oak door. It would take an explosive charge now for an intruder to get into the room. I could relax. Looking around, I admired again the magnificent ceramic stove in one corner which I had noticed earlier in the evening when changing for dinner. They must keep warm in the winter in this part of Europe. Another prominent feature was the old-fashioned four-poster double bed, complete with hangings which concealed its interior. You could have a snug time in that. Few modern hotels could offer you such princely accommodation, even if it could all do with a spring-clean and a coat of paint. There was a whiff of old-world distinction about this People's Republic. I was beginning to feel at home.

Moonlight was streaming through the open window. The summer air was balmy. The room looked out not on the town of Zenda and the valley but in the opposite westerly direction, across the moat to the ancient Castle. It was a real moat with deep water. One would not care to cross it except by the drawbridge with its formidable portcullis which still seemed to be in working order. Even in these days the Castle of Zenda was equipped to withstand a siege. Its walls rose, gaunt and black like a precipice from the rippling water. There were lights in an upper room. I wondered who would care to live in so grim a place. One could imagine only too vividly the scenes of cruelty and violence which must have occurred there when the Elphbergs ruled. With relief, I shut the window and turned back into the baroque room. The eighteenth century was more in my line. It had been a pleasant evening. A page or two of Trollope and I would be comfortably asleep.

Suddenly I heard a tiny noise. Instantly I froze. I knew where the sound had come from. My sensitive ear told me that there was somebody or something in the bed, concealed by the heavy curtains. It was an unpleasing predicament. My own security precautions had produced a boomerang effect. If attacked by the unknown person in the bed, I should never have time to unlock the door, draw the bolts and get out of the room. I had locked myself in, on the wrong side of the door. With a thrill of horror, I waited for the curtains to open. Perhaps the barrel of a gun would peep slyly out. Would it be better to rush to the curtains and fling them open myself? At least I should know my fate. This Ruritanian adventure was not what I had bargained for. I am an urban intellectual, ill-adapted by nature for danger, discomfort and nervous strain.

'I am armed,' I shouted. 'Don't move. Or I shall pump bullets into the bed. I'll be first with my burst.'

A laugh was heard from behind the curtains. Suddenly they were drawn dramatically aside. The sight I saw then came as a considerable surprise.

The arrival at Zenda that afternoon had been pleasant enough. A well-mannered, dark girl at the reception desk had welcomed me in a battery of languages and confirmed my hotel reservation.

'You are expected, Mr Mandrake,' she had said.

On the surface, that seemed only natural. I had made the advance booking from London. She was simply acknowledging the fact. But was there a slight edge to her voice? Could there be some mysterious local interest in my arrival? It was a sobering thought. I was, after all, engaged on a highly perilous secret mission. The words of a haunting nursery rhyme flashed through my fevered mind. Will you walk into my parlour said the spider to the fly? The jingle had always alarmed me. Would Zenda be for me a spider's parlour? I gave the girl one of my sharp looks, to show that I am no bumbling amateur but a sophisticated man of affairs. She riposted with a dazzling smile.

'I am Helga,' she said. 'Always at your service.'

I made a mental note of that. She insisted on showing me the fine view from the terrace on the east side of the palace opposite from the Castle. Below us lay the ancient gabled roofs of the town of Zenda with its many churches. Across the valley could be seen another large building situated on the edge of deep woods.

'That is the Castle of Tarlenheim,' she explained. 'Another of our wonderful tourist attractions. You will have heard of it, of course.'

'Tarlenheim ware. You can buy it in Harrods.'

'Exactly. The Castle used to belong to one of the ruling families before the Revolution. They had started manufacturing ceramics on their estate in the eighteenth century. Now the whole building is devoted to the State porcelain factory. Much of their production is exported. It is one of our main sources of hard currency. You know about Meissen from Germany and Herend from Hungary. Well, this is Tarlenheim from Ruritania.'

'How interesting. I expect there is a lot to see in the neighbourhood.'

'Indeed there is. Tourism is one of our high-priority growth areas. That is why they have built the Hilton in Strelsau. Here at Zenda we offer a wealth of intriguing tourist excursions. I could fix you up quite easily with a number of guided tours. Romanesque churches. High-rise low-price housing. Wild life of Zenda country. Night life of Zenda city. It all depends on your interests.'

'I'm rather keen on mediaeval castles.'

'Then you have come to the right place.'

'Is the Castle of Zenda open to the public?'

'Not usually. It houses a branch of one of the Government departments. But you are in luck, Mr Mandrake. Tomorrow night there will be a concert here of Ruritanian baroque music. It will be given in the great gallery of the Castle. You will be able to buy a ticket here.'

'I shan't miss it.'

'Just ask me for any information you need.'

'I certainly shall,' I replied, giving the girl one of my more appealing glances. It had softened many a harridan in its day.

'You are alone, Mr Mandrake?'

'I'm afraid so.'

'That is unusual. Most of our tourists come in groups and coach parties. I hope you will not be lonely.'

We exchanged signals of mutual attraction. I am by no means unused to these encounters. But it was good to feel that I had an admirer close at hand. One never knows when emergency help may be needed.

'I will have your luggage taken to your room,' she offered.

'Thank you. But I'll carry this piece myself.'

I tightly gripped my battered old brown case. How amazed Helga would have been if she had known what it contained. Only death or Lord Pargiter would part me now from the Elphberg emeralds. The elderly porter shrugged his shoulders and went off with the other case. Turning back, I saw Helga looking at me quizzically. Was there a faint hint of satire in her charming smile?

'Socialist Ruritania welcomes you to Zenda, Mr Mandrake,' she said smoothly, as if reciting a lesson. 'We hope that your stay with us will be – memorable.'

'You look English too,' said a commanding voice in my ear. 'Mind if I join you?'

It was not what I had planned. After a period of leisurely unpacking and a soporific bath, I had entered the large dining-room, looking forward to a solitary dinner with *The Last Chronicle of Barset*. There is something so calming about nineteenth-century England. It was calm I needed after the rigours of the journey to this alien land with its hidden dangers.

The voice belonged to a bouncy-looking female of hearty demeanour. With her jolly, open smile and solid figure, she could only be an English girl who had been bred from youth to outdoor sports. A younger version, in fact, of Lady Baxendale who had been the cause of my downfall at my last Embassy. I shuddered.

The girl appeared to need no invitation from me. She simply sat down. I gave her one of my frosty glances but she seemed in no way abashed.

'I'm Barbara Canterbury-Cooper,' she announced. 'Most prople call me Babs.'

'The noted show-jumper?'

'I suppose you could call me that. I mess around with horses.'

'Oliver Mandrake. From the Foreign Office.'

'I might have guessed that. You look just like a Foreign Office man.'

I found that not unflattering. Wearing one of my better tweed suits, I bore no outward signs of connection with Whitehall. Indeed I might have passed for one of the more literate of the landed gentry. But the girl had spotted me at once as a trained diplomatist. Perhaps she was more intelligent than the usual female horse enthusiast.

'We'd better order,' continued the girl. 'The service takes ages. And I'm jolly hungry.'

'I've only just arrived,' I explained. 'I don't speak Ruritanian. The menu looks quite weird.'

'I've been here for two days. So that makes me a veteran. I muddle through somehow, with lots of sign language. Ruritanian food all tastes the same. It's so highly flavoured.'

'Their cherry brandy is powerful too. That has an almost nuclear effect.'

With the aid of my companion's gift for pantomime, we managed to order a passable meal of bean soup, pork chops and curd-cheese strudel, washed down by a bottle of Zenda burgundy. I was to eat much the same thing for all my meals in Ruritania. The cuisine, though sustaining and apt to produce embonpoint over the years, is far from varied.

'What are you doing here?' asked the girl with hearty directness.

'I am just starting a holiday. Walking and old castles.'

'What fun! This is a super part of the world. Quaint villages and wonderful woods. I've been exploring.'

'Are you on holiday too, Miss Canterbury-Cooper?'

'Do call me Babs. And I shall call you Ollie.'

'Please don't. But feel free to address me as Oliver.'

'I wish I was on holiday, Oliver. But I'm really on my way to take up a job in Strelsau.'

'How strange!'

'It just came out of the blue. Of course I've competed in Moscow and I'm known on the east European circuit. That must be why they invited me to perform with the Ruritanian State Circus. They're supposed to be rather good and they've asked me to do a solo jumping item in their show. I shall also be helping with some of their own training. They want to pick my brains, such as they are.'

'Won't it be rather different from your usual round? Windsor and Badminton and all that.'

'Daddy and Mummy were a bit shocked. They thought I might go Red. But I'm not a bit interested in politics. Ruritanians have a good name in the horse world.'

'It will certainly broaden your horizon.'

'Exactly. I can't hope to do competitive jumping for ever. This will get me a foot into show business. It's a most amusing offer.'

'Will you be in Strelsau all the time?'

'Oh, no. That's part of the fun. The Circus is going on a tour of East Germany. And they want to take me with them. I shall fly home from Berlin.'

'Europe is certainly opening up these days. But don't you need horses?'

'They've gone ahead to Strelsau with my own people. They've taken the mobile caravan too. It's jolly useful. That's why I've been having my mini-holiday here. To let them settle in.

'You are indeed enterprising, Babs. But how will you manage about language?'

'No real problem. I learned a bit of German at Benenden. We had a smashing Fraülein. Educated Ruritanians all seem to speak German, even now.'

'In the nineteenth century they spoke nothing else. When Rudolf Rassendyll masqueraded for his distant cousin, the King, he must have done it all in German. But that will have changed since the Revolution. It's Ruritania for the Ruritanians these days, judging by this incomprehensible menu.'

'Isn't it gruesome, Oliver? The old German-speaking days must have been easier for us poor foreigners. Do you know, the headquarters of the Circus used to be in the Königstrasse, the main boulevard in Strelsau. Now they write me letters from a street called the Vlpszt.'

'I'm sure you can cope, Babs.'

'You sound like my games mistress at school. I was pretty fierce with a hockey stock. But animals are my real love. I've never been afraid of an animal.'

'I wish I could say the same.'

'My horses are perfectly schooled. I pride myself on that. It's just a question of discipline. All you need is plenty of love and the occasional touch of the whip. Men are just the same.'

I shuddered. This kind of dominant female is little to my taste. But it is my misfortune to have encountered several memorable specimens of the species. They seem to collect around me, like bears around a honey pot. I cannot think why, since my manner is massively dignified. My personal preference is for clinging, submissive girls with big round eyes, provided that they have some vestigial spark of spirit to lend excitement to the chase. I have met plenty of those too.

'I am no pony, Babs,' I said firmly. 'You wouldn't find me easy to control.'

The harpy laughed merrily.

'I should just love to get my hands on you,' she replied. 'You're just a big, naughty baby.'

'You've drunk too much of the local wine.'

'What about a walk in the woods after dinner?'

'No, thank you. They look damp.'

'Or a nightcap in my suite? They've given me the old oratory at the end of the east wing.'

'I'm afraid not tonight. I'm feeling rather overcome. By the journey and everything.'

'A pity. Beneath that stuffy façade, you seem really rather fun.'

To shake off Barbara, as we left the dining-room together, I retired pointedly to the library of the baroque palace. Helga had kindly informed me that it was available for the use of hotel guests. It contained no modern books but it was soothing to sit for a while looking at the old folios in their fine bindings. At least they could not talk. When at last I made my way upstairs to bed, I had the ingenious idea of using the internal telephone system to ring through to Helga. It was not too late to hope that she might still be on duty in the reception area. I would make some small complaint about needing more pillows. Perhaps she could be lured to my room. That sly smile of hers seemed a good deal more attractive than Barbara's brassy stare.

But all thoughts other than those of self-preservation were driven away when I actually entered the room and conceived in due course the appalling notion that I was not alone. When at length the curtains were drawn aside, I became aware of the identity of the thing in the four-poster bed.

It was Barbara Canterbury-Cooper, O.B.E., with very little on.

'Be jolly, Olly,' she shouted merrily.

'You gave me a terrible shock. It might have caused a heart attack. Besides, I told you before that I'm feeling rather mouldy. That pork tasted peculiar to me.'

'Nonsense. My technique is equal to all situations.'

'So I see,' I countered with dignified irony.

'I knew you wouldn't really mind. You just have to pretend to look shocked. What a time you made me wait. But at least you brought some books on the local scene. So I started to amuse myself with those. This looks rather in my line. *Reptiles of Ruritania*. With eighty full-page illustrations. What a fat volume. I never knew there were so many snakes in this neck of the woods.'

'Put it down at once please.'

'You look as if it might bite.'

'I don't like having my things messed around.'

'Selfish old bachelor, aren't you?'

'What exactly are you doing now, Barbara?'

'Isn't it obvious? Getting comfortable.'

'You should be ashamed of yourself, my girl. We represent Britain abroad.'

'On the contrary, I'm living up to one of the basic tenets of my dear old games mistress. An English gentlewoman at play should be correctly dressed for the particular sport she has in mind.'

Next morning I felt distinctly below par. After a light breakfast in my room, I hobbled downstairs. The ubiquitous Helga gave me a friendly wave from the reception desk. I returned it with a decorous nod. Women can sometimes be too much of a good thing, especially in the morning. Creeping out to a chair on the verandah, I was not best pleased.to find my way barred by the well developed form of Barbara Canterbury-Cooper.

'Now, Oliver,' she barked. 'That won't do.'

'What won't do?'

'Pretending you hardly know me.'

'But I do hardly know you, Babs.'

'After last night? That was pretty intense.'

'It has certainly left me with some extensive injuries.'

'You poor lamb! Can I look?'

'In front of all these people? Of course not.'

'You do seem a bit mottled. And there's a piece out of your ear.'

'I wish it was only that,' I retorted with some asperity. 'There are funny little bites all over my torso. And some unusually placed bruises.'

'Well, that's nothing to make a fuss about. Bruises fade. Bites heal. One has to take the rough with the smooth. You'll soon get used to my methods.'

I shuddered. I had suffered more than enough from the habits of this rampant tyrant.

'Your methods may work well on horseflesh,' I said coolly, 'but I am not a horse.'

'Don't do your stuffy Foreign Office act with me, Oliver.

40

We both know that at heart you're quite lost and helpless.'

I gave the impertinent wench one of my level stares. They have frequently been used to quell overforward subordinates.

'Kindly bear in mind,' I remarked, with massive dignity, 'that this is a public place.'

Barbara giggled.

'I thought you were more worried.' she quipped, 'about your private places.'

I resolved to cut her right out of my life.

At lunch that day I was not in one of my sweeter moods. It had been an exhausting morning following a gruelling night. In spite of my firm resolve, the wretched Babs had compelled me to take a fast walk through the Zenda woods. The terrain was uneven, the paths steep. Miss Canterbury-Cooper's ministrations required a good deal of fighting off. But I did not much relish the prospect of escaping from her and trying to make my way back to the Castle alone. Even at midday the deep forest was dark and forbidding, the haunt of wolves and wild boar. The excursion contrasted unfavourably with those nice little walks round Sevenoaks, so much enjoyed by my dear mother and aunt. I had been mad to leave England. Life abroad can be so unexpected.

I was determined to get away from Babs at lunch. So I walked straight to a table at the far end of the dining room. It was occupied mercifully by two silent men. We drank our thickly peppered vegetable soup in calm peace, undisturbed by feminine clamour.

'You must be Mandrake,' said one of the men, turning to me unexpectedly. There was power in his dark, lined face, together with a dash of sardonic humour.

'I am indeed Oliver Mandrake,' I answered simply, 'from the Foreign Office in London.'

'If I may say so, you look every inch the part. One can usually spot a compatriot.'

'Are you English too?' I asked graciously.

'Of course I am,' the man riposted. 'Isn't that obvious?'

I had clearly made a mistake. People are sensitive about

that sort of thing. But the man's voice was hard to place. It was not so much the accent as the intonation.

'I'm Gabriel Easingwold. Managing Director of Easingwold Embellishments.'

The name sounded unconvincing too, almost like a character on the stage. But wasn't Easingwold a village in Yorkshire? Perhaps he had grown up with a strong north-country accent, transmuted later into a kind of neutral speech for worldly purposes. If so, one must try to be understanding. As an experienced diplomatist, I am always aware of the need to make friends and influence people, irrespective of their social origins. I gave him one of my more gracious smiles.

'How did you know my name?' I asked.

'Saw it in the visitors' register. That girl at the reception desk is most obliging. I'm just curious and like to know about my fellow guests. When I saw there was a man from the British Foreign Office here, I thought it would do no harm to meet you. We business chaps like to have our Government behind us.'

I had been in two minds about revealing my status at the Zenda Palace Hotel. But the Ruritanian authorities would have had to know it from my visa application in any case. There is no point in telling unnecessary lies. Besides, as Easingwold had indicated, it is fairly clear from my manner that I am no stranger to the corridors of power. I could hardly have posed as a gormless vagabond.

'I am here on holiday' I explained. 'We have no diplomatic relations with Ruritania.'

'But you soon will have,' replied Gabriel Easingwold. 'I heard it on the radio. Lord Pargiter arrived in Strelsau last night to conduct negotiations. I expect Trevor Flask will be with him. He deals with this part of the world. A brilliant chap. I've heard him speak at trade promotion symposia. You know him of course?'

'We have met,' I replied with a tinge of asperity.

'Not quite your type, eh Mandrake? Well, I suppose not.' I eyed the man coolly.

'What exactly are you doing here yourself?' I asked firmly.

'Drumming up trade. For Easingwold Embellishments Limited. And consequently for Britain.'

'You export embellishments?'

'They will be going like hot cakes. The local market is taking off in a big way. Thanks to Anton here, my Ruritanian partner.'

The other man bowed silently. He was quite huge, tall and wide. Until then his face had appeared singularly devoid of emotion. But now it suddenly creased into a cheerful smile, revealing prominent white teeth. I liked him immediately. There was something engagingly honest and kindly about his expression. My sensitive antennae had telegraphed their message about Anton. He was a man on whom one could rely in a tight place. I responded with one of my friendly grins.

'What are your embellishments?' I asked the Ruritanian.

'Anton doesn't speak much English,' chimed in Easingwold. 'We're in the garden gnome field.'

'Garden gnomes! I thought they went out with the aspidistra and the anti-macassar.'

'You're behind the times, Mandrake. Garden gnomes are back. Especially in Ruritania.'

'But this country has had a revolution. It has gone communist.'

'I am not unaware of that. Even though I don't work in the Foreign Office. But the revolution was more than a generation ago. Bourgeois instincts are developing again in the socialist East. The worthy citizens of Strelsau and Zenda aim nowadays to have their flat in town and their weekend house in the country. It's all part of the status symbol urge. One must keep up with the Biedermayers. Gentrification proceeds apace.'

'No bad thing perhaps,' I commented sagely. 'Making them more like us. Blurring the edges of confrontation. The nitty-gritty of *détente*.'

'And jolly profitable too. Every weekend bungalow has a front lawn. And every front lawn needs a few gnomes. It's going to become the done thing here.'

'Little men with funny hats?'

'We have several varieties on the market. I'm thinking of starting a gnomes of Zurich series. Small capitalist goblins. One hankers also after a Karl Marx or even a Lenin. But Anton says that would not appeal to the local sense of humour. So we stick mostly to the Walt Disney conception. Perky and Grumpy, the two basic human types.'

'Are you confined to gnomes?'

43

'Oh, no. We also deal in garden statuary. We have a splendid Venus de Medici. And even a Winged Niké of Samoth-
race.'

'You amaze me, Easingwold. Life in Ruritania sounds
unusually complicated.'

'Not really. People here aren't satisfied to be just one of the
work force. They crave for a display of individuality. Hence
the flower in the buttonhole. The gnome on the lawn.'

'Very ingenious. And you travel in search of markets?'

'It's my job. Anywhere that offers the right social conditions. Once we have diplomatic relations with Ruritania,
there is bound to be a trade agreement. Then my gnomes will
flood in. The Easingwold workshops at home are poised for
victory. Unless the Common Market mucks us up. We don't
want a gnome mountain.'

'I wish you luck. But I'm afraid I have never had a lot to do
with trade.'

'I thought you probably hadn't, Mandrake. You look more
the old-fashioned type. State treaties and protocol.'

There was a tone in his voice for which I did not wholly
care.

'Protocol is not to be despised,' I retorted firmly. 'It makes
for civilized living. And it's by no means the only function of
the trained diplomatist. Some of our duties are not revealed to
the general public.'

'It's vulgar commerce that pays your salary all the same.
You diplomats are only there to help people like me. Trevor
Flask sees that clearly enough. That's why he's the type of
Foreign Office man I get on with.'

That particular heresy about diplomacy being the hand-
maiden of trade has always infuriated me. It is so belittling to
the diplomatic profession of which I am an ornament. And I
was specially irritated now to hear it coupled with the name of
my odious rival.

'I have nothing against trade,' I snapped. 'I just don't happen to find some of its practitioners very amusing.'

Easingwold frowned nastily. I felt inclined to give Anton a
wink of complicity.

'Keep your hair on, Mandrake,' retorted Easingwold.
'There's no need to get your knickers in a twist.'

'I am a senior diplomatist, Easingwold, and I am not used

to being spoken to in that way. I could get you put on the black list of the Department of Trade.'

'Oh no, you couldn't. I'm one of their growth areas. There has been talk of a knighthood. And I'm joining the Voyagers Club in Pall Mall. Haven't I seen you there, come to think of it?'

It was too much. I gave the impertinent fellow one of my reproachful glances, redolent of silent dignity. They do not usually fail.

'We could use that expression, Anton. In the gnome workshops. Just my idea of Grumpy.'

My siesta was rather troubled. Irritation acting on pastry had wreaked havoc with my digestion. So I was not best pleased to hear a tap on my door. Another visit from the irrepressible Babs would have been the final straw. But I cheered up to find that it was the mild Helga.

'Please excuse me, Mr Mandrake,' she pleaded in a low, musical voice. 'I hope I do not disturb you.'

'Far from it. Please come in.'

'Oh no, I have my duties. But I have a message for you from Professor Lemberg.'

'Who the devil is he?'

'Please, Mr Mandrake. Rude language is not encouraged in socialist Ruritania. Professor Lemberg is a scholar of great distinction. He is Director of the Zenda Museum. It's not in the Palace Hotel here but in the mediaeval Castle across the drawbridge. That's where the concert of Ruritanian baroque music will be held this evening. I mentioned it yesterday.'

'So you did. And I'm planning to go.'

'Professor Lemberg was delighted to hear that. He cherishes warm feelings towards your country. He has asked me to invite you to take a glass of mulled wine with him at the end of the concert.'

'I shall be delighted.'

'Then I will look out for you in the Castle and conduct you to the Director's suite. It is full of marvellous treasures.'

'What fun! I'm so glad you're going to be there.'

'The Castle is rarely opened to visitors, Mr Mandrake. It

has a rather special atmosphere. And our baroque music produces a unique sound. It should be an unforgettable evening.'

It was.

'How do you like our Zenda Riesling?' asked Professor Lemberg in perfect English, with a gracious inclination of his snow-white mane.

'A very tolerable little wine,' I replied with equal courtesy. 'Shy, almost furtive, but with a certain cachet.'

We stood at an open window in the Professor's elegant apartment, high up in the ancient castle keep at Zenda. Far below us blazed the lights of the old town, while across the valley the Professor pointed out the dusky shape of the Castle of Tarlenheim. A fine cabinet of Tarlenheim porcelain was only one of the treasures to be seen in the Director's private quarters. I also noted an interesting late mediaeval altar piece and some intriguing eighteenth-century portraits. Clearly the Professor was a man of authority, to judge from the state of his domain. This was how the upper classes had lived before the Revolution. It was hard to believe that we were actually in a People's Republic.

'I hope you enjoyed the concert, Mr Mandrake,' continued the Professor. 'Our music of the baroque period is rarely performed.'

I could quite understand why. It seemed to consist mainly of insipid tum-tum-tums on the lower strings, a sort of poor man's Vivaldi. But I murmured a few polite nothings. One is used to coping with all situations.

On my arrival in the music room of the Castle, I had been firmly escorted by Helga to a comfortable arm chair in the front row. She seemed to be in charge of the administration. I was by no means sorry that she so clearly recognized my distinguished status as a Government representative, albeit on holiday. The bumptious Barbara attempted to join me but was fortunately taken away to the back of the room. Gabriel Easingwold and his partner were also to be seen. I exchanged waves with Anton, who after all had said nothing to insult me. Towards Easingwold I directed one of my more freezing glances.

I took at once to Professor Lemberg, an elderly gentleman of immense distinction. When we retired to his private apartments, it was an honour to find that I was to be the only guest. That was how life ought to be lived. The public hotel for the Canterbury-Coopers and Easingwolds and other lesser people. The V.I.P. suite for the Lembergs and Mandrakes and our small world. My only regret was that the comely Helga had not been invited to pour the drinks.

'I hope you are enjoying Ruritania,' went on the Professor, with inexorable politeness.

Indeed I was. The wine was pleasant and I felt thoroughly at ease. Lemberg was clearly no dreary local official but a man of my own class, at home in the best international society. As we compared notes about the great art galleries we had visited and the famous people we had met, I found myself drawn to this sympathetic and scholarly person. My extrasensory perception had detected already in three Ruritanians, Helga, Anton and now Lemberg, qualities which might come in useful some day. I mentally earmarked them as possible allies in an emergency. My mission had begun well.

'I know what you're thinking, my dear Mr Mandrake,' said my host. 'This doesn't seem a very socialist atmosphere.'

'The thought had crossed my mind.'

'Allow me to explain. Ruritania is full of beautiful relics of the past. Nowadays they belong to the State. But we appreciate them all the more for that reason. To bring culture to the people is one of our prime aims. That is why we have regular artistic manifestations here, like the one we enjoyed this evening. The lovely things in this room have only been borrowed temporarily for study and restoration. I consider myself to be merely a guardian.'

'Like Plato's Guardians?' I asked.

'No, Mr Mandrake,' retorted the Professor with a gentle smile. 'We are not an elite society.'

I was far from convinced. Professor Lemberg might be living at public expense, but he seemed to have created for himself a singularly cosy little set-up. It was not for me to criticize. I have never been a raving egalitarian.

'And now tell me about yourself,' continued the Professor. 'Of course I know you are a British diplomat. But what made you decide to take your holiday in our country?'

I do not remember a great deal about the rest of the evening. My host plied me generously with wine and I must have talked a good deal. He seemed so pleasantly interested in my personal welfare and asked such intelligent questions. But of course I am far too wily a diplomat to have blurted out anything indiscreet. It was essential to preserve the secret of that small, but vital, item in my luggage at the hotel.

'I think you did the right thing to come by train.' commented the Professor. 'Zenda is such a delightful first stop. A flight to Strelsau airport would have been too abrupt a transition. Besides, air travel is not always satisfactory. Sometimes one's cases go astray. I prefer to keep everything with me.'

Was it imagination or did I detect a shrewd gleam behind the old gentleman's spectacles, as he bent forward to refill my glass? I am not easily deceived and have plenty of experience in avoiding pitfalls.

'In my case,' I replied firmly 'that was not a factor. I have only a few books and holiday clothes with me.'

'How sensible, Mr Mandrake. I admire those who manage to travel light. But I like to have my own small knick-knacks around me. I plead guilty to the offence of overattachment to the world of visual beauty. But I see that you too are a man of cultivated taste. Let me give you a little tour of my treasures here.'

The wine must have been unusually potent. I did not find it easy to stand up. As we walked round the room, it seemed to be moving too in a sort of circular motion.

'This little golden goblet' said the Professor, 'has a unique history. It was made at the height of the Renaissance by a forerunner of Cellini. King Matthias of Hungary gave it to the ruling Elphberg of the day, King Rudolph XI. Our monarchs are a trifle hard to disentangle because so many of them are called Rudolph. So this one is known as Rudolph the Rampant. He was not a very nice man.'

'I hope he appreciated beauty.'

'He did. In all forms. But like many rulers of the Renaissance, and indeed today, he combined connoisseurship with cruelty. He it was who enlarged the great dungeons beneath this very Castle. The flower of the land perished in his torture chambers.'

I shuddered. It was sobering to think that all this man-made beauty was constructed on a grim prison hewn out of the living rock. The Professor sensed my mood.

'Don't be nervous,' he said gaily. 'The torture chambers are no longer in use.'

Below us the lights of Zenda still twinkled. There was a moon and some friendly stars. I breathed in the warm air of the summer night.

'Now please come round to this corner,' continued the Professor. 'I want you to stand in exactly this position. From here you can see the expression on the face of Saint Jerome in the left panel of this triptych. Don't you think there is something rather curious about his eyes?'

'As if he had seen wonders.'

'Exactly. It is the face of a man who has visited the dark places of the mind. He knows how suddenly one can be transported from the upper world of beauty to the lower world of pity and fear.'

'In the midst of life, we are in death.'

'Yes indeed, dear Mr Mandrake. We all stand on the edge of the abyss.'

Something in the old man's voice should have warned me. But I jumped aside just too late.

The ground suddenly collapsed beneath my feet. It was a most unpleasant sensation, like being caught on the trap-door of a scaffold. I felt myself falling rapidly in the pitch dark. Miltonic references flashed through my bewildered mind. Was this how Lucifer had fallen? If so, would it go on for days and nights? And what would be at the bottom? A pit full of snakes or the icy waters of the moat? I felt distinctly mouldy.

My fall stopped as suddenly as it had begun. To my surprise, I found myself still standing. I was surrounded by total blackness and had no idea where I could be.

Then there was a click, as if a loudspeaker system or possibly a tape-recorder had been switched on. The cultured voice of Professor Lemberg sounded in my ear.

'Keep calm, Mr Mandrake,' he said. 'If you will take one step forward, you will find a light switch just above your left hand.'

49

He was right. The light went on to disclose a small cell cut into the rock. High above me was a little window. I must be in the dreaded dungeons below the Castle. Once again, I thought with a thrill of horror, there was a prisoner of Zenda.

'Help, help!' I shouted. 'Let me out!'

The floor behind me rose in the air, becoming level with the ceiling. I had clearly been positioned on a skilfully placed trap door, connected with an electric elevator.

The voice of the Professor sounded again, clear and cool. It was not apparent whether he could hear me or I could only hear him.

'You will be quite comfortable here for the night,' he said. 'I will explain further in the morning. There is a bed and a chair. Your pyjamas have been brought from the hotel. Don't attempt to touch the window. That could cause a disaster.

You will find an eighteenth-century chamber-pot beneath the bed. It is of the finest Tarlenheim porcelain, emblazoned with the royal arms of the House of Elphberg. We thought it might appeal. Sweet dreams, Mr Mandrake. Socialist Ruritania welcomes careful drivers.'

I awoke next morning with a splitting headache. Was it the wine or the shock? I felt understandably depressed. My vital mission to Ruritania had sustained a definite reverse. Not only was I imprisoned in the basement of a mediaeval castle, but also I had become separated from my precious charge, the Elphberg emeralds. It would be a tricky situation to explain to the Foreign Office in the unlikely event of my ever seeing them again. I cursed my folly in yielding to the blandishments of that old humbug, the Professor.

'Good morning, Mr Mandrake,' said a bright voice just behind my ear.

I looked up to see that a hatch had been opened in the wall, folding down to make a small table on which a tray had been placed. It contained a generous breakfast.

'Eat well,' continued the voice. 'Professor Lemberg thought you might like bacon and eggs.'

'Is that you, Helga?'

'Always at your service, Mr Mandrake. As I told you when we first met.'

'So you're in it too.'

'I don't know what you mean by that. I work for the directors of the hotel and the Castle. We are loyal citizens of Ruritania. And we try to do our duty.'

'You call this your duty? Trapping an innocent tourist in a rat-infested cell?'

'It is not rat-infested,' retorted Helga indignantly. 'In terms of our mass tourist industry I would describe it as an adequate individual apartment of the lower second class. And what is more, it is situated in a historic building. On commercial terms, there would be a small supplementary charge for that.'

'What's that damned thing in the window?'

'Please, Mr Mandrake. I have asked you before not to use unprogressive language. That is the famous Jacob's Ladder. It leads from earth to Heaven or Hell, as the case may be. It was mentioned in that English novel.'

'Just big enough for a body, wasn't it? Or a man?'

'That's right. When people were eliminated down here, the pipe was used to get rid of the remains. It comes out below the surface of the moat. Don't try to open it or the water will rush in and you will be drowned.'

'Still in use, I suppose?'

'Really, Mr Mandrake. That was unworthy of you. Jacob's Ladder is a relic of the wicked Elphbergs. We are in socialist Ruritania now where the death penalty is used only in extreme cases.'

'Perhaps my case *is* an extreme one.'

'I hardly think so. Probably you and the Professor will be able to straighten things out. He is so charming and clever.'

'And what about me, Helga? Aren't I charming and clever?'

'You are delightful too, Mr Mandrake. I could see that from the start. My only regret is that it should have become necessary to confine you in this way.'

'I share your regret. Why don't you let me out, darling? I'll make it worth your while.'

Through the small hatch I gave her one of my most charming smiles. It has had a dramatic effect on a fair number of young women. But this little minx only gave a silvery laugh.

'Really, Mr Mandrake. You quite underrate my devotion to

51

duty. Perhaps you are confusing me with the gaoler's daughter in 'Fidelio'. She never had her heart in the custody of the prisoners.'

'You will certainly have a fine career,' I retorted with dignity, 'in the Ruritanian prison service.'

Nevertheless I had not abandoned hope. Helga was clearly attracted by me. Something might well be built on that.

'But I was only joking,' I continued hastily. 'You're a lovely girl.'

'Thank you,' she said simply 'I like you too. You remind me of a small boy who has lost his mother. All that pushing out the chest is to conceal fear.'

'Don't you underrate me, Helga. Just you wait till the British Government hear about this. They can be terrible when they're roused.'

Suddenly a panel was drawn aside in the roof. There was a whine of machinery and then the open elevator descended. Professor Lemberg stepped off the small platform, looking spruce and self-satisfied.

'Good morning, Mr Mandrake,' he said calmly. 'Please forgive my dramatic arrival. It's rather amusing to be a *deus ex machina*.'

'I do not find the situation amusing.'

'I expected better of you. Last night you showed a spritely wit. Believe me, it was very much against my will that I took the decision to confine you here. By nature I am a man of sweetness and light. I heard you talking a moment ago about 'Fidelio'. You will remember the magical moment when the poor chained prisoners stumble out of their deep dungeons into the sunlit air. That great music of liberation has always moved me strangely.'

'I'm in no mood for cultural reminiscences,' I snapped grimly. 'When the news of this outrage gets back to London, there will be a hell of a row. I have friends in high places.'

The old charlatan's reference to 'Fidelio' had been significant. It showed that my cell was wired for sound with a speaker in the apartment above. But I was too astute an operator to reveal that I had picked up the point.

'It was a matter of stern necessity,' said the Professor calmly, 'As your namesake Oliver Cromwell remarked of Charles I. Though of course we hope that this episode will not

52

end in the same way. Incidentally, I too am not without influence at headquarters.'

'You will need plenty of that,' I shouted. 'Do you really understand what you have done? At the very moment when your benighted country has embarked on negotiations to resume diplomatic relations with Britain, you decoy to your abode a distinguished British diplomat who happens to be enjoying a well-deserved holiday. Lulling his suspicions with a lot of bogus cultural chat, you then forcibly and treacherously convey him to a hateful dungeon well below the waterline. There you hold him against his will, in the face of the strongest possible protestations of innocence. You're for the high jump, Lemberg. And in double quick time.'

The Professor blenched.

'I shall be able to explain,' he gulped. 'I acted in the national interest. It was my duty to detain a foreigner who was acting so strangely. I have telephoned a full report to Strelsau.'

'All that business about Saint Jerome. It was a most deceitful way to behave.'

'Well, at that hour of night, I could hardly invite you to step down into the dungeons, could I? At least there was no unseemly argument. I do hate the use of force. This seemed the most civilized method.'

'So you and your female accomplice are alone in this enterprise?' I asked hopefully. Helga's face had disappeared and the hatch had shut.

'Far from it, Mr Mandrake. We have several experienced strong men in the Castle. But they are not cultivated and I like to keep them out of the way. Don't get the wrong idea though. Any attempt to escape would be most unwise. Do you see that hole in the hatch? It contains the barrel of a gun. And behind it is the admirable Helga. She has taken a course in marksmanship as well as in hotel management.'

'She's got the wrong target this time.'

'I'm sorry it had to end like this, Mr Mandrake. Our chat last night was most enjoyable.'

'But it was all a deception. You're no professor. You're just a secret policeman.'

A spasm of chagrin passed over Lemberg's finely chiselled profile.

53

'That is a complete slander,' he shouted. 'Of course I'm a professor. I have held the Chair of Fine Arts at Zenda University for twenty years. And I'm not a complete fool. How could I hold down this job and enjoy these privileges if I didn't co-operate with the authorities? In any case,' he added more cautiously, 'I do so most willingly. I'm a loyal citizen. It is my duty to assist the Office of State Security. They have made me one of the leading custodians of the Zenda sector. It fits well with my position here at the Castle.'

'Oh, most convenient,' I said sarcastically. 'Now your comforts are a good deal easier to understand.'

'I'm sorry you take that cynical attitude, Mr Mandrake. I had hoped we might be friends. I am primarily a scholar, a connoisseur and a *bon viveur*.'

'With a connoisseur's capacity for cruelty?'

'Only if provoked. I acted last night in self defence. If I had not detained you, someone else would. And that would have meant a black mark on my dossier. I'm an old man, Oliver. This Castle is my world. I have no family, only the artistic treasures here. I could not face the thought of losing them.'

I looked him straight in the eyes and saw that he spoke the truth. It is one of my gifts.

'You have forgotten one consideration, Professor,' I said more gently. 'There are other English people in the Zenda Palace Hotel. They will have noticed my absence today. The alarm has probably been raised already.'

'Fortunately not. Fortunate for you, I mean, as well as for me. If things began to go wrong, I should be forced to take – extreme steps.'

There was something about this placid intellectual which I found distinctly alarming. I did not care to visualize his extreme steps.

'Helga has behaved admirably,' added the Professor. 'With her customary presence of mind, she has persuaded your compatriots that you are in excellent hands. I have taken you on a two day trip to see a particularly beautiful mediaeval chapel in the mountains. The man Easingwold and the woman Barbara exchanged jokes at your expense. By tomorrow they will all have left Zenda. They have absolutely no idea of your whereabouts.'

'Just wait till it's discovered,' I said. 'The world press will

54

go to town. There will be nasty pictures and headlines. Debonair diplomat in dismal dungeon.'

'I wouldn't call it a dungeon,' replied Lemberg evasively. 'As the excellent Helga has tried to explain. But I agree that it could do with some brightening up. I might send down some of those attractive coloured prints. Heroes and heroines of the Ruritanian Revolution. I couldn't spare any of the antiques. Damp can be fatal to them.'

'It could be fatal to me too.'

'This is no time for self pity, Oliver. I want you to enjoy my company while it lasts. Lie down on the bed please and then I shall feel free to take the chair. That's better.'

'Still within range.'

'I suppose your bitterness is understandable. I still haven't explained why you are here.'

'You certainly haven't.'

'Well, to put it bluntly, your behaviour since arriving in our country has been quite extraordinary. The reports have been almost flooding in.'

'What reports?'

'My dear Oliver, nobody could be as simple as you sound. Don't you realize that our system for surveying the activities of suspicious persons has been brought to a peak of perfection? You have been under surveillance from the start. Even at the frontier you acted oddly. You were extraordinarily nervous when confronted with the customs officials. It was clear that you were deeply preoccupied with the safety of one particular suitcase.'

I remembered the dear old lady on the train who had given me so warm a welcome to Ruritania. She must have been one of them.

'On your arrival at the Zenda Palace Hotel,' continued Lemberg, 'you showed a similar anxiety. In fact you insisted on carrying one of the cases yourself, to the surprise of the head porter. He happens to be an honest patriot. Naturally the hotel staff became interested in your activities. They observed the frequency with which you kept retiring to your room, presumably to check on the safety of your baggage.'

'They're a disgusting bunch of snoopers,' I blurted out. 'And that goes for your precious Helga too.'

'My dear Oliver, please keep calm. I thought they taught

55

you self-control at those British public schools. By the way, it would be civilized if you would call me Amadeus. My parents were devotees of the divine Mozart.'

'You know nothing about me,' I growled.

'That is the whole trouble. We know either too much or too little. It is perfectly obvious that you have smuggled something important into the country. That was why I invited you last night. Under the influence of alcohol, you revealed the existence of an extremely guilty conscience. Of course we have made a thorough search of your luggage. But nothing has been found.'

'I thought so,' I shouted triumphantly. 'That proves my innocence.'

'On the contrary, Oliver, it has made us all the more worried. If we had detected drugs, currency, even pornography, we should have shrugged our shoulders. We do not want trouble with British diplomats, particularly when there are negotiations with your country. But since there is a complete mystery, I feel it my duty to unravel it. I have asked for instructions from Strelsau. Maybe they will be able to guess what you have brought illegally to my country.'

My heart sank. Lemberg might not know of my connection with the Elphberg emeralds. But in Strelsau they might well put two and two together, with devastating effect.

'Of course it would help a great deal,' continued the Professor, 'if you would make a full confession, here and now.'

'Certainly not,' I shrieked. 'I am completely innocent.'

'Then you offer me no alternative. I am obliged to detain you here until word is received from the capital. Then, if cleared, you will be allowed to proceed. Meanwhile, we shall do our best to make you comfortable. Helga has organized a tasty dumpling stew for your lunch. Knowing your intellectual interests, I thought you might enjoy starting work on this Ruritanian grammer. It is not an easy language. There are five separate forms of subjunctive. But it would be a great thrill to read our sagas in the original.'

'You're trying to drive me mad, Amadeus.'

'Don't be childish, Oliver.'

'What happens if they decide to dispose of me? Will I be shot or strangled? I'd like a clean death.'

'My dear boy, you are quite absurd. That's the trouble with

56

you old-fashioned capitalists. You actually believe your own propaganda. You face nothing worse than a possible charge of illegal importation of artefacts into Ruritania. Nowadays the penalty is quite mild, only fifteen years' imprisonment. And with remission for good conduct, you could be out in a mere twelve years.'

I groaned. Which of my current girlfriends would still be attractive in twelve years? I might even have lost some of my own drawing power.

'Imprisonment here is much less rigorous than it used to be,' continued Lemberg in soothing tones. 'Our aim is to improve the criminal and return him to society as a reformed character. There is great emphasis on remedial therapy. That is why I am anxious for you to start learning our language.'

'So you assume that I'm guilty?'

'I assume nothing, my dear Oliver. Ruritania is a civilized, modern country, governed by the rule of law. A few years in one of our hygienic penitentaries could be a novel experience.'

'I should prefer death.'

Lemberg's glasses glittered.

'People often talk like that,' he said. 'But I don't think you would.'

I had been escorted up to the Professor's apartment at the point of Helga's competent gun. It was evening once more. The summer night blazed with the stars of Zenda.

'How nice to see you again, Oliver.' said the Professor warmly. 'I hope you passed a peaceful day. Now I want you to meet a very dear friend of mine. This is Dr Gertrude Markovitz, one of our most distinguished medical experts.'

The lady doctor was not young but her face was full of character. With her budding moustache, she had the makings of a good-natured walrus. There was, however, something sinister about her appearance at this low point in my fortunes.

'Keep your hands off me!' I shrieked. 'I won't take an injection.'

'You have been reading too many spy thrillers, Mr Mandrake,' said the female medico in a pleasant light baritone. 'I am here to help you.'

'Dr Markovitz has come today from Strelsau' explained Lemberg. 'But until recently she was living in your country. Our excellent Cultural Relations Institute had arranged a year's exchange visit for her. She is a great lover of the British.'

'Do you know Hampstead, Mr Mandrake? Keats Grove. The Spaniards. The Bull and Bush.'

'Yes, of course I do. But that doesn't make me a fit subject for medical experiment.'

'I am not a surgeon, Mr Mandrake. Have no fear.'

'Dr Markovitz is an eminent psychiatrist.'

'Just as I feared! She's come to certify me. You're going to lock me up in a loony bin.'

'Really, Oliver, you are quite absurd. Benevolence is our watch-word in socialist Ruritania. I think it will be best for me to leave the two of you together. Fifteen minutes with Dr Markovitz can do much to heal the troubled spirit.'

'I'm not troubled.'

'Aren't we all?' replied the Professor calmly. 'By the way, I should not advise you to jump out of the open window. It's a long way to the ground.'

'Isn't Amadeus a remarkable man?' said Dr Markovitz, when the door had closed on him.

'That's one way of putting it,' I answered drily.

'You must try to work with us. We are your friends. Why don't you make yourself comfortable on this couch? And feel free to call me Gertrude.'

'What on earth is the point of all this mumbo-jumbo?'

'We think you would benefit from a little analysis. There is no point in wasting time until instructions are received from the Ministry. About your disposal, I mean.'

'My disposal?' I yelled.

'Just a way of putting things. Pardon my bad English. My special field is one in which Amadeus thinks you could use help.'

'And what is that?'

'Sex therapy. I have been successful in curing many potential offenders.'

'I find that damned offensive, Dr Markovitz. Unless you are trying to play some kind of macabre joke.'

'You are not a very young man. And yet you remain a bachelor.'

58

'What's so funny about that? My sex life is entirely satisfactory. And I happen to be robustly normal.'

'Who is normal, Oliver? May I call you that? In my professional opinion, nobody is wholly normal. Just as nobody is wholly sane.'

'That may well be true of your patients, Madam, by the time you have finished with them.'

'It is strange though that you have never married.'

'I never found a girl who came quite up to scratch.'

'Perhaps you make the mistake of putting women on a pedestal. Like Dante and his Beatrice.'

'Far from it. I've had quite a down to earth love life. Girls seem to go for me. Like wasps around the honey-pot.'

'Oh, I see. You're the philanderer type. Proud of your virility and your prowess. Rather boastful on the subject in fact. That usually masks a deep sexual insecurity. No doubt you have secret fears of impotence. Coupled possibly with a submerged homosexual streak.'

'Stuff and nonsense,' I shouted. 'This is all balderdash.'

'Your strong reaction at my mention of homosexuality is an interesting indication. I should like to follow that further. Do you have a mother to whom you are much attached?'

'As a matter of fact, I do. Is that a crime?'

'And perhaps another elderly female relative? With a well-developed personality?'

'You could certainly describe my Aunt Margot in that way.'

'And no doubt you attended one of those famous British boarding schools? Where you were cooped up for months at a time with other adolescent boys.'

'What if I did, Dr Markovitz? I'm afraid you're constructing a fantasy.'

'I observe with interest that you do not appear to view me as an attractively mature woman. There is something lacking there. We girls usually know when a man is capable of making a fully virile response.'

'I'm aroused quickly enough by pretty girls. Have you compared notes with Helga?'

'It may interest you to know,' snapped the doctor in a considerably less friendly tone, 'that many of my patients fall madly in love with me. In fact that is what I consider to be the normal and healthy reaction to a course of sexual therapy. But feel free to go your own way. You will undoubtedly find out from experience that, in the absence of regular conjugal visiting, properly controlled therapy in my special field can have a most soothing effect. During a period of prolonged imprisonment, I mean.'

'So you think I'll get a long sentence?'

'Amadeus thought I should prepare you for the worst.'

'You are perfectly beastly people. And your penal system offers a prospect of infinite boredom.'

'On the contrary, it could be the making of you. I could turn you from a twisted branch into a fine, tall tree. Now, it would help me to make clinical notes if you would kindly start describing your sex life. From the beginning. When did you first notice that little girls are different from little boys?'

'That would take some time.'

'Naturally. But I am here to listen.'

I had only got as far as the episode of Matron's scarlet knickers when Professor Lemberg burst into the room. He was clearly in a state of some excitement.

'You have been fooling us all, Oliver.' he said. 'I am really quite cross with you. The authorities in Strelsau have sent me a long message of explanation.'

'What on earth do you mean?'

'They have guessed your secret. If you have smuggled something into our country illegally, it can only be one thing. You must be bringing the Elphberg emeralds. Possibly the Rassendyll ruby too.'

'It's not true,' I shouted. 'I deny the charge completely. The Brigadier would never part with his bloody ruby.'

'I see you are well informed, Oliver. That is significant. The British move is obvious. You have brought the gems to assist Lord Pargiter in his negotiations. Your story about a holiday was never at all convincing.'

'He is a sort of human diplomatic bag.' said Gertrude with a nasty giggle. I eyed her icily.

'Now you must understand,' continued Lemberg, 'that these stones are the crown jewels of Ruritania. We need to get our hands on them straight away. Then they can never be used by Lord Pargiter and his mission to extract concessions from us against our will. As a patriot I must obey my instructions. They are of the highest possible priority.'

'You will never get them out of me.'

'Don't be so sure, Oliver.'

'You searched my luggage. You found nothing.'

'That only proves that you have the gems on your person.'

'Shall I search him?' suggested Gertrude gleefully. 'Perhaps he should be strapped down first.'

'No, you will find nothing that way,' said the old man. 'The Foreign Office in London are diabolically clever. But Strelsau have spotted the ruse of the wily British. The Elphberg emeralds are not on Mr Mandrake's richly developed body. They are inside it.'

'Bloody rot!' I shouted.

'You note his fury. It constitutes further proof. The trick is an old one. It is much used by diamond smugglers in South Africa. The stones are taken out of their settings and encased in tiny bags of wafer-thin plastic. Then the carrier just swallows them. In that way they can remain hidden in the stomach for hours or even days. A good dose of castor oil and they become visible again.'

'You might give him an emetic,' suggested Dr Gertrude helpfully. 'Plain mustard can be very effective if taken in large quantities. Alternatively, you could use a strong enema.'

'Certainly not,' I shrieked. 'If you behave like that to a senior British diplomatist, you will feel the full weight of the displeasure of Her Majesty's Government.'

'Of course it may not be enough,' continued the female harpy. 'It might be necessary to employ a stomach pump. Or even have recourse to abdominal surgery.'

My heart sank. I cursed that foolish meddler, Sir Edmund Byfield, now living comfortably in peaceful England. How little he had done to prepare me for the horrors of the stomach pump.

'We have no time to lose, Gertrude my dear,' said the Professor. 'Strelsau have emphasized that. I had better send for the strong men. Then you can get going with the syringe and pump.'

'You seem to forget, Amadeus, that I am a highly qualified psychiatrist. To ask me to do this kind of work is like employing a Rolls Royce to draw a load of coal. Besides, I lack the necessary manual dexterity.'

'Your attitude is noted, Gertrude. With regret. In the hour

of national crisis, all patriotic citizens have to pull together. But I suppose there's no help for it. I shall just have to seek emergency aid from the Zenda General Hospital.'

'Not at this hour of night,' said Gertrude. 'They'll all be drunk. They would make the most awful mess of our poor British guest. Strelsau wouldn't like that.'

'Then first thing in the morning. Unless by then Oliver can give us some further clue.'

I thought of the morning with shuddering distaste. With it would come the syringe, the pump and the rusty scalpel.

'And now let's relax,' added the Professor with ghastly jollity. 'What about a little Mozart? Gertrude is particularly fond of the Requiem.'

'You might both come to take a look at the expression on Saint Jerome's face,' I suggested. 'It's just a question of standing in exactly the right position.'

'Ah, that famous British sense of humour,' commented Gertrude gaily. 'It is indeed unique.'

No wonder I had a nightmare that evening.

I was attending a State Dinner at Buckingham Palace. Full evening dress and decorations were the order of the day. Tiaras too, for the ladies. I noted the distinguished Foreign Office representation, consisting of the Foreign Secretary himself, Lord Pargiter and Sir Edmund Byfield. How gratifying that I too should be included among the honoured great. With a tinge of self-satisfaction I straightened my white tie. Then I glanced down. With a thrill of horror I realized that I was naked from the waist downwards. In an agony of apprehension I turned an enquiring gaze on Sir Edmund Byfield.

'It's all right, my dear Oliver,' he murmured. 'Your appearance is perfectly correct in the circumstances. You see, you have been prepared for abdominal surgery.'

I awoke with a surge of relief to realize that it had all been a hideous dream. And then realization flooded over me of the ghastly prospect which was in fact in store for me. My tormentors were determined to get the Elphberg emeralds out of me by hook or crook. Or rather by syringe or pump. But they would not succeed because the damned things weren't inside me at all. The only hope was to tell them quickly how to find the jewels, presumably still hidden in the secret compartment in my luggage at the hotel. But that would be a betrayal of my trust. The Foreign Office would be furious. Bang would go my hopes of promotion. It was an appalling dilemma. I felt distinctly low.

That was when I started to hear the sound. It seemed to come from outside the window, where the pipe called Jacob's Ladder went up to join the moat. I skipped out of bed and snapped on the light. With a thrill of horror I realized what was happening. That rhythmic tapping could mean only one thing. Someone must be in the pipe. It would be a frogman who had come from the moat. He was working to file away the iron bars which protected the exterior of the window. Then he would shatter the glass pane and try to enter my cell.

But there was a fatal flaw in the plan. Helga had warned me that the pipe came out below the surface of the moat. If I tried to open the window, the water would rush in and I would be drowned. Perhaps that was what the person in the pipe intended. I was to be secretly murdered and my body sent up to the dark waters of the moat. Thus another unhappy prisoner would leave the Castle of Zenda.

'Stop!' I shrieked. 'Stop!'

My only hope now was that Professor Lemberg or Dr Markovitz would hear me through their electronic equipment. Their threatened surgical ministrations, though deeply unattractive, would be preferable to the watery fate now in store for me. Any second now and the filthy fluid would pour in, rising to my mouth and my nostrils, filling my throat and lungs, causing me to splutter and choke and die. It would be a nasty way to go.

'Help, help!' I yelled. 'Amadeus! Gertrude!'

I thought of my dear old mother and aunt. I thought of Debbie at home and all those lovely girls I would never fondle again. I thought of my career and the knighthood I would not now attain. I thought of Trevor Flask and wished most sincerely that he could have taken my place.

With a sickening tinkle the glass suddenly shattered. Broken panes from the window fell into the room. Beyond I could see the now severed bars. I braced myself for immortality.

But it was air and not water which surged into my cell. It took me a moment to realize that I was not, after all, going to die that night. Relief and mystification overwhelmed my sorely tried brain. Suddenly I realized that a figure had emerged from the pipe and was climbing in through the window. It must be the man who had shattered the bars. He was dressed from head to foot in a wet suit of the type used by divers and his face was covered by a mask. Once again a terrible fear gripped me. The fact that I had not drowned did not mean that I was safe. It was more than likely that this mysterious, muffled man had come to murder me. A quick thrust of the knife and my contribution to British diplomatic technique would be a thing of the past.

In a final, despairing move I summoned up my remaining strength and gave a loud and prolonged scream. The effect was quite blood-curdling. I hoped that it would frighten Professor Lemberg out of his elderly wits, wherever he might be reposing.

'Shut up, Mandrake, you fool,' said the unknown intruder. 'I'm on your side.'

The voice seemed slightly familiar, even through the mask. But I was too bewildered to be able to work out who it might belong to. Life in Ruritania was proving awfully confusing, even to a trained diplomatist like myself.

The mystery man turned back towards the window.

'Follow me quickly,' he snapped.

'But I can't,' I expostulated. 'I'm too wide. I shall get stuck in the pipe.'

'You go first then. It's your only hope.'

There was no time for argument. I cursed the cruel fate which condemned me, a peace-loving sybarite, to participate in so foolhardy an adventure. At school I had even avoided the Sea Scouts because I preferred to keep my feet dry. And now I was being invited to enter a moat at midnight, beneath a mediaeval castle in a sinister foreign country. It was not my kind of thing at all.

'I hope I can trust you,' I said to my would-be rescuer. But I knew that I had no alternative.

Bracing myself for fresh horrors, I crawled through the window and entered the pipe. Now I was in the notorious Jacob's Ladder on my way to Heaven or to Hell. It proved to be a shade less narrow than I had feared. Slowly I managed to wriggle my way upwards, assisted by some vigorous shoves from the mystery man. At one point I thought I really was stuck. Panic surged over me and I felt a strong urge to blubber. But a special push from below liberated me again. Eventually I felt the air coming down more freely and realized that we must be near the top of the pipe.

When at last I stuck my head out, it was to look down on the unappetising waters of the Zenda moat. Now the explanation of my unexpected delivery from drowning was revealed. The minx Helga had deceived me. The pipe came out not just below the waterline but just above it. No doubt my captors had misled me on purpose so that I would not interfere with the window. Nothing in Ruritania seemed at all simple.

'Jump out, you ass,' shouted a voice from below. It sounded a bit like the voice of Hamlet's father, beneath the platform at Elsinore.

'It looks so cold,' I moaned. 'And so wet.'

'Hurry,' yelled the muffled voice. 'We shall be followed.'

Suddenly I felt myself seized from below by the feet and projected violently upwards. Unable to recover balance, I was pushed over the edge of the pipe and toppled forward into the inky water. It was a far from pleasing sensation. Sobbing with fear and shock, I found myself struggling to keep my head above the chilly current of the moat with its unpleasingly mediaeval odour.

I think I might have drowned, even then. It had all been too much for me and I could not take any more. But my strange rescuer swam briskly towards me, and held me up, and guided me towards the shore. There were lights there and people and I gathered they were on our side. I was too confused to understand fully what was happening. But I realized that we had to make haste and move secretly for fear of the pursuit. Professor Lemberg would be implacable once he realized that I had gone. The whole strength of the highly centralized Ruritanian State would be launched against me. I was still in the most deadly peril.

The next hour or two passed like a dream. All I can remember is that I was held on horseback by muffled figures and thus escorted by secret ways through the Zenda woods. I felt distinctly mouldy. But it had penetrated at last into my consciousness that I was now in friendly hands. I was tired and muddled but I was beginning to get dry. The luck of the Mandrakes had held again.

It was daybreak and the birds were singing merrily in the great beech trees when we came at last to a lonely house in the middle of the forest. Dazed though I was, my trained observation told me that this was probably one of the hunting lodges which ringed the Castle of Zenda in Elphberg times. It looked dilapidated but it was secret and secure. My spirits rose as my strange companions ushered me into a large hall profusely decorated with antlers of stag and tusk of boar. I was given a comfortable pullover and a mug of warm coffee. I began to feel quite human again.

The leader of the rescue team, the mysterious frogman who had invaded my cell, had kept his face covered with a stocking-mask throughout our ride through the woods. Now he unveiled his face and gave me a sardonic grin. I responded with a gasp of surprise. It was none other than Gabriel Easingwold.

'That gave you a shock,' he remarked with a somewhat superior smile.

I assented with quiet dignity.

'I thought you dealt in garden gnomes,' I observed.

'And in human life.'

'I owe you mine,' I replied simply. 'And I am duly grateful.'

Another masked figure divested itself of its headdress. It proved to be Anton, Easingwold's huge Ruritanian partner. We exchanged friendly grins. I felt a trifle reassured.

'I'm still bewildered,' I continued.

'Of course you are, Mandrake. But you mustn't overstretch your mental powers. I'll try to explain.'

I smiled wanly. Even the trained intelligence of an experienced diplomatist could not withstand these constant sudden shocks. Events moved more slowly in Whitehall. I like to be ahead of the game, not behind it.

'So you're on my side?' I asked.

'Of course I am,' replied Easingwold cordially. 'I was sent out from home to look after you.'

Relief flooded over me. So I had not, after all, been abandoned alone and defenceless in the grim Castle of Zenda, at the mercy of a ruthless connoisseur and a sex-crazed female psychiatrist. The British Government, bless them, had been behind me all along. It was typical of Sir Edmund Byfield, with his meticulous efficiency, to arrange this discreet and highly welcome form of protection. I might have known that I should not be entirely unguarded on this vital mission.

'I tried to hint to you,' continued my preserver. 'Back at the hotel. Don't you remember? I mentioned that I knew Trevor Flask.'

So it was really Flask to whom I owed this timely rescue. The thought was not entirely welcome. But at least the fellow's brain had been deployed to good effect on my behalf on this occasion.

'You didn't give the impression then,' I said, 'of being on my side. In fact you were distinctly rude.'

'I'm sorry about that,' replied Easingwold casually. 'But it was necessary. For cover purposes. I didn't trust Lemberg from the start. Or any of his staff.'

I felt somewhat uneasy. Lemberg had certainly deceived me, in spite of my long diplomatic training. I must be more cautious in future.

Anton appeared and put before me a steaming plate of bacon and eggs. I eyed him gratefully. It was good to get another satisfactory breakfast under the belt.

'Eat up, my dear Mandrake,' said Easingwold cheerfully. 'We want you to feel well.'

He was a decent chap after all. I had quite misjudged him.

'How did you know where I was?' I asked.

'Miss Canterbury-Cooper mentioned that you had disappeared. She seemed to be missing you acutely. We weren't fooled by the Professor's story. Anton is a Zenda man. And the rest of our party are gypsies living in these woods. We knew about the dungeon of Zenda. You could hardly be anywhere else.'

'I'm most awfully grateful, Easingwold.'

'All in the day's work, Mandrake. We have contacts in the Castle. I couldn't bear to think of you in the hands of those fiends. They would have done nasty things to your digestive tract. You must keep well away from them now.'

'Won't you be in danger too?'

'I'm not associated with your disappearance. The garden gnomes business provides excellent cover. It's perfectly genuine, by the way. That's why I can travel so freely.'

'I can't help admiring you,' I burst out with generous enthusiasm. 'You think of everything.'

Easingwold responded warmly.

'Thanks, old man. I've got a lot of experience. It's just different from yours.'

I had begun to feel distinctly more cheerful even though my rather good suit had been somewhat damaged in my passage through the pipe and the moat. The competent Easingwold could take care of things from now on. This strange half-world of intrigue and deceit, in which I now unwittingly found myself, was more in his line than mine. It was his job to protect me until we could get the emeralds through to Strelsau.

'Take that business of the pipe.' continued Gabriel affably. 'I should never have been fooled by that story about its coming out below the water level.'

'Why not?' I countered with dignity.

'Because I've had a scientific education. Unlike you chaps in the Foreign Office. The pipe was originally built so that dead bodies could be sent up to the moat. But you could never get a body up through the pipe against the pressure of water flowing in the opposite direction. That's why it had to come out in air, not in water.'

'Indeed?' I countered calmly. Easingwold might have saved my life. But there was no need to dwell on the circumstances.

'Where is my luggage?' I continued. 'I should like to change my clothes. My collar is below standard.'

'Poor old Mandrake,' laughed Gabriel. 'You're not really prepared for rough living.'

'I am certainly not,' I responded testily. 'I am a highly experienced diplomatist. Not the hero of some frivolous adventure novel.'

'Well, keep quite calm. Your luggage is in fact here. We brought it for you from the hotel.'

'That was kind.'

'Not at all, Mandrake. It was essential.'

'Essential?'

'Certainly. As you well know. The Elphberg emeralds are concealed in your baggage. Thank heavens that old Lemberg never found them.'

My delicate antennae swung into action. So Easingwold knew the whole story of my secret mission. I suppose it had been necessary to brief him fully, if he was to give me the necessary protection.

'Here are your cases,' continued Easingwold. 'Let's have a look straight away and make sure the emeralds are safe.'

I felt some embarrassment at this suggestion. The Foreign Office had impressed upon me the importance of not revealing the secret of the hiding-place to anyone. On the other hand, Gabriel Easingwold was clearly reliable. Had he not risked his life to rescue me from the horrors of the Castle of Zenda? He naturally shared my anxiety to know about the safety of the gems.

'Is this the right place?' I asked nervously. 'Suppose one of the gypsies sees us?'

'They won't talk. Anton has them under control.'

'I think I'd like a bath first. And a change of underclothes.'

'Nonsense, Mandrake. This is no time for frivolity.'

Easingwold eyed me sternly. I was beginning to find him rather alarming. But I didn't want to lose his good-will. With the Ruritanian authorities on my trail, he represented the only hope of my getting out of the country alive.

'Open your cases,' he said firmly, 'and show me the emeralds.'

With the slightly smug air of a successful conjuror, I took out my thick and heavy copy of Pollard's zoological master-piece, *Reptiles of Ruritania*. It had been lying casually in my room in the Zenda Palace Hotel.

'The inner pages of this book have been taken out,' I announced with quiet dignity. 'And the Elphberg emeralds are there instead.'

'Well, get on with it,' snapped Easingwold. He and Anton were craning forward, their eyes shining with excitement. I could not blame them. It would be a dramatic moment, this first glimpse of the crown jewels on their return to Ruritania. The suspense for us all was almost unbearable.

I undid the elaborate clasp on the solidly bound old book and flung it open. The secret compartment was there all right. But it was empty.

'Where are they?' shouted Easingwold.

'Gone!' I shrieked.

'You perfect bloody fool!' yelled Easingwold, losing all control. 'You great booby!'

'I will not be spoken to in that way.' I said with massive dignity. 'I am a senior official of the Foreign Office. Your language will be reported on our return to London.'

Easingwold saw that he had gone too far. But he still scowled at me in a decidedy unpleasant manner.

'You lost the emeralds,' he growled reproachfully.

'I did not lose them,' I retorted neatly. 'They were taken. While I was in the dungeon.'

'Not by me. And not by Lemberg's men. They told you so, Mandrake.'

'Then by someone else.'

'I should like to know who,' murmured Easingwold with a touch of menace.

It was all most confusing. My long diplomatic experience had not prepared me for the labyrinths of Ruritanian intrigue.

'The Foreign Office will be furious,' I commented. 'And Lord Pargiter too.'

I could not afford to have another failure chalked up against my name. Lorenzo Fontwell of the Personnel Department had made that only too clear. The whole episode would be tricky to explain.

'I also am furious,' said Easingwold.

'You're supposed to protect me,' I pointed out. 'We're in this together.'

'We'll have to move on quickly,' said Easingwold with an air of decision. 'This place is too near to the Castle of Zenda. Lemberg's men will be searching the woods. I suppose I might do better without you now. You're not exactly a physical asset in these adventures. And your face is too well known. Whereas the authorities have nothing against Anton and me.'

Panic seized me.

'Don't leave me,' I pleaded. 'Please take me with you. My mission has failed. I just want to get out of this country as quickly as possible. I'm not at all well. That swim in the moat has given me a heavy cold.'

'Poor old Mandrake,' murmured my protector. 'You really are a pathetic sight. I won't abandon you. But you must obey my instructions. However bizarre they may seem.'

'To the letter.'

Gabriel and Anton took me to the back of the shooting lodge where a truck was parked. It contained two large coloured figures made of papier mâché.

'What on earth are these?' I asked.

'Garden gnomes, of course. Part of our collection of samples. These are the jumbo variety. Very popular for collective farms. They are conveniently hollow. So you will be able to travel inside one of them.'

'Won't that be uncomfortable?'

'Yes. But less so than having Dr Markovitz stick syringes up your behind.'

'Where are we going?'

'That will become apparent in due course.'

'Can I trust you, Easingwold?'

'You have no real alternative.'

I glanced at Anton's friendly features. He was beckoning towards the grotesque gnomes.

'Anton wants to know which gnome you would prefer to travel in. It's a choice between Perky and Grumpy.'

'In my present mood,' I replied with quiet dignity, 'Grumpy would suit me better.'

'It was not a pleasant journey,' I commented.

'I never said it would be,' snapped Easingwold. 'But you're a man on the run.'

'I had awful cramp in my left leg.'

'Better than electrodes on the genitals. Really, Mandrake, you have no guts at all.'

I stared at the fellow rather coolly. But I could not afford to quarrel with him now. The situation was too desperate. If I could only get out of the country and communicate with the Foreign Office, it would be up to them to warn Lord Pargiter in Strelsau about what had gone wrong with the emeralds. I imagined his reaction. And Trevor Flask, who had never cared for me, would hardly help.

'It's not very nice,' I added ruefully, 'sneezing inside a gnome.'

'Buck up, Mandrake. You've got more fun ahead of you.'

'Where are we now?'

'On the other side of the Zenda valley. In the Castle of Tarlenheim.'

'Not another bloody mediaeval castle?'

'An eighteenth-century one this time. A fine example of the Ruritanian baroque. Liszt once spent a weekend here.'

'The faithless Helga pointed it out to me,' I said weakly. 'It houses the State porcelain factory. The place is the size of a battleship.'

'Exactly. A nice harmless institution. Quite devoid of dungeons.'

'What happens here?' I asked.

'We rest and recuperate. Fortunately I have good contacts with the factory. There's some talk of producing hand-painted porcelain versions of my more artistic gnomes. For the North American market. At Tarlenheim they're keen on developing contacts with foreign buyers and with the other great European ceramics places like Meissen and Herend. It's a circuit of its own, the porcelain world. That's why they have these nice guest rooms in the Castle. We're in one of them now.'

'I think I'll have a quiet rest,' I announced. 'For about a week.'

'Nonsense, Mandrake, this is no moment to flag. You've got to live up to your cover.'

'What cover?'

'Anton and I have told the management here that you are a distinguished foreign buyer. You represent a big London store in the vicinity of Sloane Square. We're about to embark on a conducted tour of the factory. It's the only way to avoid suspicion.'

'Won't I be recognized?'

'Quick as a flash, aren't you, Mandrake? Just pop this false beard and moustache on. One should never travel without them. I've got the spirit gum here. There's no need to preen yourself in front of the mirror.'

I looked decidedly distinguished with the full beard, like some intrepid African explorer of the Victorian age. Perhaps it would be a style worth adopting at home. If indeed I ever got home.

Easingwold, Anton and I were welcomed in the Manager's office at the factory by a civil female guide. The gypsies had mercifully disappeared.

I was impressed by the cleanliness and efficiency of the porcelain manufacture. The material was conveyed on a belt which moved slowly round the huge room. The guide spoke in clear English and I decided that I had better appear interested.

'The moulded figures are placed on the moving belt,' she explained. 'As you see, some of them are quite big, like this soup tureen. The belt takes them automatically into the furnace for the first firing at a temperature of one thousand degrees Centigrade. This gives the material its first glaze.'

'Stand well back from the furnace,' whispered Easingwold to me. 'It's terribly hot. We don't want an accident.'

'Painting of the porcelain can begin after the first firing,' continued the guide. 'The conveyor belt brings the material to this section where our painting ladies get to work. They cannot be rushed, so the belt has to move very slowly. This method is known as underglaze decoration. It is a speciality of Tarlenheim.'

'Most artistic,' I murmured graciously. Some of the young girl painters would have repaid closer inspection in happier times.

'Now the material is being slowly conveyed into another furnace,' continued the guide. 'This one is even hotter. The second firing is at one thousand, four hundred degrees Centigrade. Further decoration is then applied on the fired and glazed porcelain. The results are automatically conveyed to our despatch section for export.'

'An ingenious combination,' commented Easingwold, 'of handwork and mass production. The operatives are mostly girls, I observe.'

'Except at the furnaces. That is a job for strong men.'

'Do you have a night shift?'

'I am afraid not. In socialist Ruritania the workers value their family life too much. And their evenings with the State television service.'

'Then you have to shut down production,' said Easingwold, 'after the day shift goes home.'

'Yes, indeed,' replied the guide. 'The conveyor belt is naturally stopped. The main switch is just up there. I always point that out to visitors, in case of emergencies.'

'What about the two sets of furnaces?' asked Easingwold.

His interest seemed to be almost overdone.

'We keep the fires going all night,' replied our guide. 'That is cheaper than starting them again each morning. You see, intense heat is needed.'

'We have greatly enjoyed our visit,' said Easingwold graciously.

'Perhaps you will come now to the Manager's office. We should like to present you with some Tarlenheim figures as a souvenir of your visit.'

As we left the production line, I saw several of the girls looking at me with interest. Pensively I stroked my magnificent new beard. I was beginning to feel a little better. A romp with the Tarlenheim work force could have been an amusing experience.

Back in the castle guest room I looked enquiringly at Easingwold.

'Our hosts have agreed that we may all stay the night here,' he said. 'Other rooms have been assigned to Anton and myself. So you can tuck down quite cosily here for the evening.'

'What about dinner?' I asked.

'No provision for that, I'm afraid. You had an excellent breakfast.'

'But that was hours ago.'

'Really, Mandrake, you're priceless. Not at all the type I would have chosen for this escapade. Have a swig from this brandy flask.'

It tasted good but bitter. I sank back on the bed. It had all been too much. At least Tarlenheim was an improvement on Zenda. Or so it seemed then. In a moment I was asleep.

I awoke to a distinct sensation of unease. My sensitive powers of perception told me at once that something was wrong. I was lying on a hard surface which projected uncomfortably into my back. And I could not move my hands or my feet, my waist or my head. It was more or less dark. But there could be no doubt that I was efficiently strapped to some unyielding object.

'Help!' I shouted. 'Help!'

'Shut up, you great booby,' hissed Easingwold's grating voice in my ear. A light snapped on.

'Where am I?' I asked.

'On the conveyor belt of the Tarlenheim factory.'

'How did that happen?'

'We put you there.'

'What on earth for?'

'A very good reason, my dear Mandrake. Which I shall now have the pleasure of explaining to you.'

My heart sank. His voice did not sound at all friendly.

'You are now in the underglaze decoration section,' continued Easingwold more affably. 'Between the first and the second firing. As you know, the furnaces burn all night. And the belt moves slowly in this section to allow for the hand painting.'

'It doesn't move at night,' I said. 'They turn it off.'

'It can be turned on,' snapped Easingwold. 'They obligingly showed us the switch.'

'What would be the point of that?'

'You will be conveyed, slowly but inexorably, towards the furnace. As you may remember, the second firing is at one thousand, four hundred degrees Centigrade.'

'That's hot.' I said. 'I don't think I should survive.'

'Well done, Mandrake. You got the point pretty quickly.'

'It seems so unnecessary.'

'On the contrary. It is an essential operation. You need to disappear. Right out of the reach of Lemberg and his merry men. And you will. A dignified diplomatic figure, neatly fired and glazed, will arrive in the despatch section tomorrow morning. They might be able to sell you to Fortnum and Mason.'

'But I shall be dead.'

'Yes, Mandrake, you will be very dead.'

'I thought you were on my side.'

'That was your mistake. Get this into your tiny brain. I am not on your side.'

'Who are you working for then?'

'Myself.'

'But I don't understand.'

'Poor Mandrake, you understand so little.'

'What was the point then of rescuing me from Professor Lemberg?'

'I hoped you would be able to tell me how to get the emeralds out of your luggage. But you failed. So you became highly expendable.'

'It's all so confusing.'

'It won't last long.'

'Anton will never allow you to do this to me. He's a decent human being.'

'I wouldn't rely on that. He rather enjoys this kind of thing. In fact it's for his sake that we have mounted this little performance. Show him, Anton.'

Anton's large, comfortable face swam into my ken. But his expression had changed. The benevolent look, which had always reassured me, had gone. Instead I found myself staring up at the false grin of a jovial sadist. Pursing his lips, he spat on my forehead with a gesture of disgust.

'You were quite wrong to put your trust in Anton,' continued Easingwold pleasantly. 'He has some nasty ways of causing men to die. This is one of the milder ones.'

Tears of baffled rage welled from my eyes and coursed down on to my false moustache. My extrasensory perception, usually so reliable, had failed me badly in the case of the burly Ruritanian.

'You won't get away with this, Easingwold,' I snapped.

'Why shouldn't I? I'm taking off your beard. Hope it doesn't tickle. The man found dead in the plant tomorrow won't be the same as the one I brought here this afternoon. There is nothing to link us together.'

'I still don't understand. You're not working for Ruritania. And you're not working for Britain. It's all so complicated.'

'Don't fret, Mandrake. Your last hours should be spent dwelling on eternity. I'm turning on the current now. Quite gentle, isn't it? You are hardly moving. But about three hours will get you into the furnace. Once inside, you won't last long. But I don't envy you the hours of waiting. It will be in the dark.'

'I shall scream.'

'Nobody will hear.'

'The conveyor belt is meant for small ceramic objects. The furnace door won't take me.'

'Oh yes, it will. It can hold a soup tureen. Your stomach is no higher than that.'

'You're a vile beast. I'll get you black-balled at the Voyagers. I'm on the Election Committee.'

'Dear old Mandrake! Well, I can't chat any longer. Need my own sleep. Don't get over-optimistic if it takes time. It's midnight now and you should be inside by three. The morning shift doesn't start until six. You'll be well glazed by then. You'll know when it's going to happen. The soles of your feet will get hotter and hotter. As you approach the furnace door.'

The light snapped off. I felt decidedly below par. Nothing in my diplomatic experience had prepared me for catastrophe on so Wagnerian a scale.

Easingwold had been inaccurate on one point. It was not entirely dark. There was a dull glow from the glazing furnaces. But that was not in itself encouraging. It showed that the damned furnaces were working. The conveyor belt was operating too. I could feel it throbbing quietly underneath me. The diabolical scheme was bound to succeed. Within three hours I should be exposed to temperatures of one thousand, four hundred degrees Centigrade. It would be an unusual termination to the career of a member of Her Britannic Majesty's Diplomatic Service. With bitter regret I thought of my main motives for joining the Service; good food and drink, comfortable foreign travel, social cachet, an opportunity to hob-nob with the ruling few, public recognition by the Crown. Now instead I faced a gruesome and lonely death in flames, owing to the bungling mismanagement of Sir Edmund Byfield and the fools and knaves in the Foreign Office. For their absurd plan they should have chosen the oafish Trevor Flask rather than an attractive and charming officer like myself, for whom women would weep in three continents. I felt tempted to give some robust yells and screams. But nobody would hear. Instead I found myself sobbing pitifully from misery and fear.

There could be no doubt about it now. Minutes and panic-filled hours had passed. I would be near the point of no return. The conveyor belt had moved me remorselessly forward. The glow of the furnace seemed nearer now. And the soles of my feet were becoming decidedly warmer. It could not just be imagination. I was approaching the furnace door. But for my good Jermyn Street shoes and my socks from Hamper and Hartpole, my sensitive soles would already be painfully scorched. The moment when my ankles entered the flames hardly bore thinking about. Presumably I would perish of suffocation pretty soon. But there would be some moments of agony first. The full horror of the fate in store for me struck through my imagination like a knife through butter. It was no moment for heroics. I have never pretended to be rugged, and I don't like getting my lower limbs wet, much less fired and glazed. I heard myself giving a piercing shriek.

There were voices, people running. A light snapped on. A voice shouted.

'He's here.'

Was I in Heaven? If so, it was a relief, though not a surprise, to hear that they spoke English there.

'Is that you? Oliver Mandrake?' asked a voice in my ear.

'Yes,' I murmured.

'What on earth are you doing? Is this an attempt at suicide?'

'Certainly not,' I snapped. 'Do you think I'm lying here for fun? They tied me up.'

'These straps are too complicated,' said another voice. 'It would take ten minutes to untie them'

'But he'll be inside the furnace in three minutes.'

'A pity,' commented the second voice. 'He had potential.'

'An interesting past. But not much of a future.'

'Help!' I yelled. 'Save me!' It was a relief that the unspeakable Easingwold had not gagged me, trusting no doubt that my death screams would be heard only by the owls of Tarlenheim.

'Is there really nothing we can do? He looks so awfully helpless.'

'The switch!' I shrieked. 'To stop the mechanism. It's on the wall behind you.'

They found it. The throbbing ceased. I was stationary.

'Just in time,' said a voice. 'He had about two minutes left.'

Relief and exhaustion swept over me. Life in Ruritania was becoming simply too hectic for a *bon viveur* of literary tastes. I fainted.

'My dear Lord Pargiter,' I said, 'I can explain everything, if you will be good enough to listen. I may have appeared to be duped by that odious Professor Lemberg. I may also have seemed to be hoodwinked by the loathsome Gabriel Easingwold. But I knew what I was doing all the time. I am a diplomatic operator of long experience and I am not easily fooled. You will note with satisfaction that I came through my ghastly experiences unscathed. Oliver Mandrake is alive. That is what matters, isn't it? In the circumstances, I cannot see why you are kicking up such a fuss about the temporary disappearance of a few paltry stones. You must see matters in perspective, Lord Pargiter. And you too, Sir Edmund Byfield. Oliver Mandrake is restored to his loving colleagues. We will celebrate with a rather quick luncheon at the Voyagers.'

'You're rambling, Oliver,' said a female voice.

'So would you, whoever you are,' I retorted, 'if you had been so nearly roasted alive.'

'Poor old Oliver!'

'I seem to know that laugh.'

'We have met.'

'Who the devil are you?'

'Sit up and see.'

I did so. The shock was considerable. There were two people at my bedside. Those long arrogant noses and that flaming red hair were only too familiar. I was staring into the mildly mocking faces of Flavia and Henry Rassendyll.

'Oh Heavens!' I moaned. 'Not you again.'

'We saved your life,' said Flavia mildly.

'I am grateful,' I responded with dignity. 'You seem to make a habit of preserving poor old Mandrake. Last time it was dogs in Sussex. Now it's flaming furnaces in Ruritania.'

'We like to look after you.'

'But can I trust you, Flavia? My memories of our earlier meeting are not entirely happy. You threw me across the room and nearly broke my back.'

'It was your fault. You were unduly saucy.'

'Whose side are you on? That's what I'd like to know.'

'Yours of course, Oliver dear. Let me spell it out since you are in a state of shock. We are on your side.'

'That's what Easingwold said. But he wasn't.'

'Poor old Oliver, it's all been too much for you. Daddy

79

warned you not to get involved with Ruritania. It's not a simple country.'

'Why are you both here? I thought you were with the Opposition? Are you in danger here too?'

'We'll explain when you feel better,' said Henry impatiently.

'Henry is quite right,' commented Flavia more gently. 'Your mental powers are not up to further disclosures. We don't want to unhinge your mind. You must have a long rest.'

'I'm too upset to sleep,' I protested.

'Henry will give you some vigorous massage. He's awfully good with horses.'

'I'd prefer to have the massage from you, Flavia. It would be more fun.'

'Oh, all right. But no nonsense this time. Kindly remember that I'm almost a princess.'

Her hands were indeed soothing. I had not slept properly for two nights. The bed was old-fashioned and comfortable. I passed into a dreamless sleep.

'Not another damned mediaeval castle!' I said peevishly. 'This is the final straw.'

'This is no run of the mill castle.' snapped Flavia as she motioned me to the breakfast table in a huge timbered hall. 'You are in the Castle of Elphberg. Much older than Zenda or Strelsau. The cradle of our House.'

'But it's a ruin. I read that in the guidebook on Ruritania.'

'That would be one way of describing it. There are admittedly some holes in the roof. But part of the building can be just about lived in. I wouldn't care to be here in winter though. The wind must howl down through the mountains.'

'What will you eat?' asked Henry in a breezy, practical manner. 'There's venison or boar's flesh or pig's trotters.'

'A lightly-boiled egg please. I like mine done for precisely three minutes.'

The meal was brought by an ancient retainer, with a gnarled face and villainous grin. He reminded me of one of those British character actors of the old school who spend so much of the day in the bar at the Garrick Club.

'This is Karl,' explained Flavia. 'His family have been with us for the last seven hundred years.'

'I don't understand a thing.' I said unhappily. 'What is Gabriel Easingwold playing at? Why are you here? And how can you be living in the Castle of Elphberg? I thought this country had become a socialist republic. It's all so bloody confusing. It would make everything so much easier if I knew who is on my side. And who is not.'

'We are on your side,' said Flavia simply. 'As I told you, and showed you, last night. Come and sit on the terrace when you've finished. We'll have a nice talk.'

The view from the terrace was superb, even more sensational than that from the Castle of Zenda. We were clearly high up, somewhere in the remote hills. No other building was in sight. The vegetation was much sparser than in the Zenda-Tarlenheim valley. For mile after mile the mountains curved away into the blue distance. In spite of the summer weather, pure snow caps covered the highest and most inaccessible peaks. I gasped at the sheer beauty of the scene.

'Where are we?' I asked. 'A long way from Tarlenheim, I hope.'

'Yes indeed,' replied Flavia. Henry had disappeared, which I did not particularly regret. 'Elphberg is situated in one of the most remote mountain regions of Ruritania. We brought you here in the station-wagon but you were unconscious for most of the time. Far across the snow line you would come to the frontier with Romania. It's the same chain of hills which forms part of the Carpathian mountains in Transylvania.'

'Very scenic,' I murmured. 'But tell me about Easingwold.'

'He is a thoroughly bad man.'

'I *had* noticed that, Flavia.'

'You may not know that he is a Ruritanian by birth.'

'Good Heavens! That explains his accent, or at least his intonation. I spotted that it wasn't quite English.'

'How clever of you, Oliver. I don't think you would be able to pronounce his real name. We have known about him for some years. He came to England, pretending to be a refugee from the communist Government here. You know how easy it is to take advantage of the good nature of the British and their sentimental attachment to exiles. Then he started to build up his export business, dealing in those absurd garden gnomes.

They seem so ridiculous that nobody takes him very seriously. That is what he wants. His real interests are political, or rather criminal. We have to watch such people carefully. They are traitors to the royalist movement in exile, which is naturally led by my House.'

'So he is really an agent for the communist Government in Strelsau?'

'Not at all. Gabriel is working against the governments of both Ruritania and Britain.'

'But I don't understand.'

'I knew you wouldn't find it easy, Oliver. The trouble is that mentally you haven't moved forward in time. You're still living in the old days of the Cold War, almost like my father in his different way. You think in traditional terms of the capitalist governments of western Europe and the communist governments of eastern Europe as if they necessarily always had conflicting interests. But we live now in an era of *détente* and co-operation. I don't need to tell you that. That's why Lord Pargiter is negotiating in Strelsau. London and Strelsau are seeking a better relationship.'

'As I am well aware,' I interjected with dignity.

'What you forget is that *détente* does not suit everybody. Some people, even if they are a small minority, disapprove of understandings between capitalism and communism.'

'You mean the extreme Right? People like your father?'

'No, the opposite. The extreme Left.'

'But the Ruritanian Government *are* the extreme Left.'

'Not to people like Gabriel. He and his friends believe that the Ruritanian Government are traitors to the sacred cause of Marxist-Leninism. He sees Professor Lemberg living in style in his museum while others of the ruling elite purchase garden gnomes or dine with Lord Pargiter at the Strelsau Hilton. He regards this process of becoming the new bourgeoisie as a betrayal of the dictatorship of the proletariat. He hopes to stir up the class war and fan the flames of international revolution. In other words, he and his friends want to be the bosses.'

'They sound thoroughly dangerous.'

'Of course they are. That's what I'm trying to make you understand, Oliver. Gabriel's group will stick at nothing. His friend Anton is a sinister killer. They are in touch with fanatical terrorist cells in other countries. Their aim in Ruritania is to discredit the regime. In fact they are the enemies of all stable European governments.'

'I still don't understand what they have got against me.'

'Gabriel wants to see bad relations between London and Strelsau. It's part of his opposition to *détente*. So he's out to wreck Lord Pargiter's mission. He knows how much this depends on the peaceful hand-over of the Elphberg emeralds which you are carrying out to Strelsau. So his aim is to seize the emeralds and hide or destroy them. Then he will blame the British Government for bad faith, thus causing Pargiter's mission to fail. This will help to foment the class war and the revolutionary struggle.'

'I had no idea about this additional complication. They never briefed me in the Foreign Office.'

'Your people are not very strong on Ruritanian politics. That's why they need diplomatic relations. I should advise you to keep well clear of Gabriel Easingwold in future.'

'I have every intention of doing so. As well as being a sadistic murderer, he is certainly a most convincing liar. After rescuing me from the Castle of Zenda, he tried to persuade me that he is on my side. I almost showed him where the emeralds are hidden.'

'But you didn't?'

'Oh, no. I was not born yesterday.'

Some instinct of self-preservation made me withhold from the bewitching Flavia the vital information that the emeralds had in fact already been lost or stolen. I had learned from bitter experience that nobody in Ruritania was to be trusted.

'We were sure that you had told Gabriel nothing,' said Flavia. 'That was why he decided to murder you in such a spectacular way. You were very brave to stand up to him for so long.'

'Thank you, my dear,' I answered with simple dignity. 'I only did my duty.'

'Thank God we got to you in time.'

'Yes indeed,' I replied with a shudder.

'Your secret might have died with you. Ruritania would have lost her crown jewels for ever.'

'So that's all that matters to you, Flavia! You don't care about me at all.'

'I'm getting quite fond of you, Oliver. But we are naturally interested in the emeralds. That is indeed why we risked our lives to get hold of you. Poor old Lemberg has been relieved of his post. They're searching for you all over the country.'

'I've no sympathy with Amadeus Lemberg. He's a baroque bore. But will I be safe here?'

'Of course. It's miles from anywhere. Nobody will just come by chance. And we are your friends.'

'Can I be sure of that, Flavia?'

'You knew, when we first met in Sussex, that I found you rather amusing. My father and brother both said you were effete. But I guessed you might have – hidden depths.'

'You weren't very responsive.'

'I panicked. But here in Ruritania the blood flows more freely. Things could be – different.'

There was no mistaking the hint of invitation in the girl's low, musical voice. I felt deeply stirred.

Halcyon prospects opened up and I gave her one of my most beguiling glances.

'Let's explore the Castle,' I said hastily. 'Do you live in a turret?'

'Keep it cool, Oliver. Remember I'm on home ground. There will be a time and place for everything. And now Karl wants to know what we will drink before lunch. A glass of old Elphberg brandy perhaps? It tastes not unlike turpentine.'

'I would prefer Pimms Number One,' I replied calmly. 'If you happen to have the ingredients in so remote a spot.'

'Certainly. That's why we travel by station-wagon. To bring out our English comforts. Henry insists on them.'

The drink was excellent, the summer morning benign. The snow on the high hills gleamed remotely white and pure.
Sparkling too was the vivacious face of this intelligent and sensuous girl. I felt at peace with the world.

'I still don't understand,' I said, 'how you have managed to follow me so closely.'

'We started to take an interest in you,' replied Flavia, 'when you came to see Daddy in Sussex. Then we heard about your subsequent intriguing performance here. That old lady in the train was once my Nanny. And young Helga at the Zenda Palace Hotel comes from a long line of Royal grooms. One of Easingwold's gypsies is in fact Professor of Indigenous Art at the University of Zenda. His grandfather was the court painter.'

'But I thought they all reported to State Security?'

'Everyone in Ruritania reports to State Security. But there is still much loyalty to the House of Elphberg. And now let us eat.'

At the door of the dining room, Flavia turned towards me.

'Now you will meet your host,' she said. 'You should bow before shaking hands.'

I was swept into the great chamber. There was no time for further enquiry. An elderly man came forward to greet me. He had a kind, quizzical face.

'Cousin Michael,' said Flavia in English. 'May I have the honour of presenting Mr Mandrake? Oliver, you are in the presence of His Majesty The King of Ruritania.'

I was somewhat taken back but I managed to bow with my customary aplomb. The King led Flavia into luncheon, followed by Henry and myself.

'The table is only laid for four,' said the King.

'That's what I explained to you, Cousin Michael,' interjected Flavia smoothly. 'We shall be four in number.'

'Then he's not coming to table?'

'No.'

Henry glanced at me quickly, though Flavia remained impassive. With my quick powers of perception I received the distinct impression that our host had made a mistake. Somebody else was in the Castle. Somebody who was not to eat meals with us. Somebody whose presence was not supposed to be disclosed to me. Through what fresh quicksands might I not be walking? But I was steeped now in the horror of Ruritanian adventure and would not be caught so easily a third time.

The meal, served by the doddery Karl, was tolerably good, though somewhat spicy for my taste. Outside the glorious mountain peaks made a dramatic backdrop. They, at least, were genuine.

'I drink to your health, Mr Mandrake,' said our royal host. 'I hope you like our imperial Elphberg wine. There are still a few bottles left in a remote part of the cellars.'

The wine tasted strangely, almost as if there had been a tinge of blood in the grapes.

'They say this wine tastes of blood,' said Henry as if he could read my thoughts.

'Not inappropriately,' commented Flavia. 'We are in the heart of traditional vampire country here.'

'I thought the vampire legend derives historically from Transylvania,' I said. 'Wasn't there a rather nasty ruler there called Vlad the Impaler, also known as Dracul?'

'He lived only just across the mountains,' explained our host. 'Beyond the snows. Dracul was a cousin of the Elphbergs. The Elphberg ruler of his day was Alberic the Unspeakable. They are supposed to have shared strange tastes.'

I smiled politely but inwardly I shuddered. It was just my luck to have been spirited away by an ancient family occupying an almost ruined castle in an area traditionally frequented by vampires and werewolves. Nostalgically I thought of less arduous continental trips, taken with my dear mother and aunt to little watering places in the vicinity of Dieppe.

'Every ruling family has its opponents,' put in Flavia smoothly. 'It was natural for people to accuse the mediaeval Elphbergs of consorting with vampires and werewolves and traffickers in black magic. But they had to do something to pass the time. Up here the winter nights must have seemed very long.'

The unusual wine had produced a not unpleasing effect. I began to feel a sensation of wellbeing. After all, it was not every day that one ate a meal with one of the crowned heads of Europe. It would be an experience to dine out on in after years. Admittedly, the old boy's title was a bit shaky and presumably he never had actually been crowned. But as head of the family, he would be in direct lineal descent from Queen Flavia. Old-style legitimists would certainly accept him, even if the present Government of the Ruritanian People's Republic refused to do so. But why on earth was he allowed to live like this? It was all most mysterious.

'Poor Oliver, you looked so bewildered,' said Flavia kindly. 'Perhaps we ought to explain. Cousin Michael is the lawful king of Ruritania. People who want to compromise call him the Archduke Michael. But to the communists in Strelsau he is Mr Elphberg or State Employee No 23,642.'

'Why do they let him remain here?'

'It happens to suit them. The tourist trade is very important to Ruritania. It brings in a lot of much-needed foreign currency. But the western tourists are much less interested in the marvels of modern industry than in the seamier side of Ruritanian history. The wicked Elphbergs are a particular source of macabre fascination. The State Tourist Bureau runs regular buses up here from the Strelsau Hilton. In fact a party will be coming tomorrow. They call them Alberic Tours since the emphasis is on the eccentricities of our ancestor, Alberic the Unspeakable. In Romania they have similarly attractive Dracula tours. The Strelsau party spend about two hours here. They are offered refreshment and are shown the dungeons and torture chambers.'

'Not more torture chambers!' I gasped.

'Every Elphberg castle had its torture chambers,' said Flavia. 'They were standard equipment.'

'But the King?' I asked. 'What does he do?'

'He is the star turn,' replied Flavia bitterly. 'The chief attraction for the gaping tourists. In this way the authorities both keep their cake and eat it. Cousin Michael is the officially designated custodian of the Castle of Elphberg, for which he receives a modest salary from the State. By employing him in this way the State hope to cut him down to size and reduce his potential as a focus for discontent. At the same time he brings in a lot of money for the tourist industry. The visitors love being escorted round by a king, especially if they are Americans. And the State gains international kudos by allowing the Elphbergs to live in Ruritania at all. It's a sophisticated policy.'

'They seem to allow you to pay visits from England too?'

'It's part of the deal. Henry and I like to come every summer. Henry's mad on the shooting. It's some of the wildest in Europe. But Daddy seldom bothers.'

Henry and the Archduke Michael, as it seemed sensible to think of him, were deep in converse at the other end of the table. I turned quietly to the lovely Flavia.

'I get the impression,' I said, 'that you are more realistic than your father and perhaps your brother. Your father is so bitterly opposed to the socialist Republic. But you seem more willing to compromise.'

'One has to live in the real world. Not everything done since the revolution has been bad.'

I smiled at the girl invitingly. What a superb Diplomatic Service wife she would make, I thought. And to be married to an Elphberg would immeasurably increase one's own prestige. No more postings after that to disagreeable countries outside the chandelier circuit.

Suddenly Henry Rassendyll, who had drunk deeply throughout the meal, turned in my direction.

'I know what you're thinking, Mandrake,' he almost snarled. 'It's all damned degrading for a King of Ruritania.'

'I suppose so,' I answered faintly.

'You may be right,' said our host mildly. 'But it's one better than starving or even living in a working-class tower-block in Strelsau. At least I am on home ground here. And some of the foreign ladies are really rather sweet. They even give me the occasional tip in hard currency.'

'I think we have the makings of a deal,' said Flavia. She had declined my pressing invitation to join me in an afternoon siesta but had agreed that we should stroll in the flowery meadows round the Castle before dinner. The golden light of evening shone on the distant peaks.

'What exactly have you in mind?' I asked.

'You want to spend the night with me.'

'It would be perfect bliss.'

'And I need something from you in exchange.'

'What is that, my darling girl?'

'I want to know where you have hidden the Elphberg emeralds.'

'What makes you so sure about that?'

'You must have. You haven't got them on you. Henry has searched. And no-one else has found them.'

'I've got to get the emeralds to Strelsau. Lord Pargiter must hand them over to the Government.'

'Don't worry about that, Oliver. Contrary to what my father told you in England, we now accept that the Ruritanian crown jewels must be returned to the present Ruritanian Government. Anything else would be too dangerous for our family. After all, poor Cousin Michael is a State employee.'

'I'm glad you're being sensible.'

'The question is who should get the credit for returning the emeralds. If Lord Pargiter does so, the British Government will gain the kudos. But they are far away and it doesn't matter much to them. It would be better if the Elphberg family could be the donors. After all, they do really belong to us. Then Cousin Michael might get better treatment. And Anglo-Ruritanian relations would still benefit.'

I could see the sense in her suggestion. But of course I couldn't really help her, since I had no idea where the damned gems actually were. I was determined, however, not to reveal this unfortunate state of affairs to the Elphberg-Rassendyll family at the present time. I could not help remembering how brutally Easingwold had treated me once he realized I was no longer useful to him. My one hope of safety at the Castle of Elphberg lay in being considered indispensable.

'I know what we'll do,' I said with one of my winning smiles. 'We'll have a night of love together. And at dawn I'll tell you my secret.'

'Done,' replied the young princess. 'It will be a variation on the Arabian Nights theme. You won't let me down?'

'On my honour.'

'Your honour as an English gentleman. That's enough for me.'

I felt rather a cad. But there would be some fun first before the hour of reckoning came.

'Oliver darling.'

'Yes, my beloved.'

'What exactly are you doing?'

'Admiring your beautiful breasts.'

'It's funny. I had a distinct impression that you were trying to creep towards your clothes.'

'Just a trick of the early morning light.'

'There would be no point in trying to sprint for the door. The castle gates are all locked. And the dogs are loose.'

'I never want to leave you, Flavia.'

'It must be dawn now.'

'I suppose so.'

'I hope you enjoyed our night of rapture.'

'It was certainly memorable.'

'You sound a little dubious.'

'I think you may have done something rather serious to the veins in my neck. There's red on the pillow.'

'Did I bite you a bit, darling? It is one of my habits. But I did warn you that we Elphbergs have vampire blood in our veins. When in Rome, do as the Romans do, you know.'

'I feel rather faint. I may have lost a lot of blood.'

'Probably not more than half a pint. I thought you had a taste for the exotic.'

The girl was a fiend in human shape. My only desire was to escape as soon as possible. I would prefer to take my chance with the dogs.

'Poor old Oliver! I'm afraid I'm too highly flavoured for you. But I'll make it up to you. I'm going to give you a rather lovely present.'

'Not more bites please! I don't care for them at all.'

'Calm yourself, darling. It's just something in a small box.'

'What on earth is it?'

'Open it.'

'Good God. It's a fantastic stone. It can't be?'

'Yes, Oliver, it is. You are holding the Rassendyll ruby.'

'But how on earth did you get it?'

'I took it from Daddy's study at home.'

'Won't he be furious?'

'Probably. But then he always is.'

'What am I supposed to do with this?'

'Hand it to Lord Pargiter. He can give it to the Ruritanian Government. That will help to compensate him for not being able to donate the emeralds.'

'I don't understand. You're so keen about getting the emeralds. Yet you let me have the ruby.'

'It's quite simple. The emeralds are the Ruritanian crown jewels. They ought to be handed over by Cousin Michael. The ruby is Rassendyll family property. It doesn't have the same historic associations as the emeralds. I don't want to make the British Government look a fool. After all, I'm British too. Let them offer the ruby and we will donate the emeralds. Then we all benefit.'

'Very sensible. You're a great girl.'

My spirits rose. Despite the loss of the emeralds, it would be a distinct consolation to be able to offer the Rassendyll ruby to the notoriously testy Lord Pargiter.

'And now, dearest Oliver,' said Flavia sweetly, 'the dawn has come. It is your turn to keep a promise. Just where are the Elphberg emeralds?'

'I haven't the vaguest idea,' I replied calmly.

A moment later I shrieked in pain and horror as the little princess went for my jugular vein.

'You owe us an explanation, Mr Mandrake,' said the Archduke Michael in a voice of icy calm. It was two hours later. The three of them were facing me across the refectory table in the great hall. The Royal Pretender sat flanked on one side by the unsympathetic Henry Rassendyll and, on the other, by an implacable Flavia. The atmosphere was that of a drum-head court-martial. After so memorable a night, I felt distinctly groggy.

'I have already told you all I know,' I said wearily. 'The emeralds were stolen from me by some person unknown. I cannot tell you where they are now.'

'We don't believe you,' snapped Henry. 'You promised my sister. Were you deliberately trying to deceive her then?'

'He broke his promise,' said Flavia. 'And now he must pay the penalty.'

'I only wish I could help you,' I remarked urbanely. 'After all, you did rescue me from that horrible Easingwold. But I'm afraid we are just wasting time. I think I'll leave you now. A nice walk to the bottom of the hill will do me good. Don't bother about breakfast.'

'You would be most unwise to try to leave the Castle of Elphberg,' said the Archduke. 'The dogs are loose. We keep them to protect us from the wolves, which are vicious in this locality.'

'Mr Mandrake likes dogs,' commented Henry, with an unpleasant sneer.

'You can't keep me here against my will,' I almost shrieked.

'There is an alternative,' said Henry. 'To put you outside the Castle gates and see what happens.'

Suddenly the door was flung open.

'Where is he?' shouted a deep voice at the end of the hall. 'Where is the beast Mandrake? The villain who violated the honour of our precious Flavia.'

A figure advanced towards us. With a thrill of horror I recognized the identity of the new arrival. It was none other than Brigadier Rudolph Rassendyll.

Archduke Michael turned towards me.

'You have met my English cousin?' he enquired politely.

I remembered only too vividly my unsuccessful visit to his estate in Sussex.

The Brigadier rushed up to me and seized me violently by the throat. I shrieked in agony. Flavia's bites had left nasty scars, now covered by a rough bandage. Henry restrained his father, none too gently.

'Rapist!' yelled the Brigadier. 'Flavia has told us all. You seduced our precious lamb, taking advantage of her purity and innocence.'

'That's pretty rich,' I remarked. 'I'd like to see anyone raping Flavia. Just look at what she has done to my throat.'

'That was self-defence,' said Flavia primly. I gave the deceitful girl one of my icy stares.

'She was willing,' I continued. 'Even enthusiastic.'

'Liar!' shrieked the Brigadier. 'You have fornicated with a female member of the House of Elphberg-Rassendyll. For that you die the death.'

'Calm yourself, dear cousin,' said the Archduke. 'As the English say, there is no point in crying over spilled milk. Our main concern now is to get the emeralds.'

'Unfortunately,' added Henry, 'Mandrake won't talk.'

'I'll make him talk,' snapped the Brigadier. 'I can make anyone talk. I have my methods.'

'We know about your methods,' said Henry to his father. 'Don't go too far this time.'

With a sudden flash of enlightenment, I realized that I had perpetrated a terrible mistake. I should have made it clear to the Rassendylls from the start that I knew nothing about the whereabouts of the damned emeralds. Then they might have left me alone. Now they would never believe me.

The Brigadier was staring at me with anticipatory malevolence, like a cat examining a rather juicy mouse. I shuddered.

But where had he come from? Had he arrived during the night? It was more likely that he was the mysterious personage whose existence in the Castle I had suspected the day before. If so, why had his presence been deliberately concealed from me? I was soon to learn.

Flavia put a hand on my arm.

'You had better try to calm him,' she said, indicating her father. 'We don't want him to go berserk.'

'He is berserk already,' I remarked.

'Not by his standards. This is only the early stage.'

I shuddered.

'What do you suggest?' I asked.

'Come clean with us. We know you know. I explained it all last night. Once we have the emeralds, we shall simply hand them over to the Government of Ruritania. Nothing will be lost to the British side.'

'What's that about the emeralds?' screeched the Brigadier. 'We'll get them out of Mandrake all right. And then we'll take them straight back to dear old England. That's where they belong now, with the Rassendyll branch. Out of reach of the filthy scoundrels who pretend to rule Ruritania.'

'Lower your voice, dear cousin.' said the old Archduke mildly. 'Remember I have to live here.'

I felt quite bewildered.

'But Flavia promised me,' I protested. 'She said that, if I helped you, the gems would be delivered in Strelsau.'

'Stuff and nonsense!' said the Brigadier. 'The girl has been fooling you. That has never been our plan.'

I looked reproachfully at Flavia.

'Is that true?' I asked.

'I had to make you feel that handing over the emeralds to us would not really harm British interests. That was to make things easier for you, Oliver.'

'So you deceived me, Flavia.'

'And you fooled me.'

'Well, our deal is off,' I said. 'Neither side has a right to complain.'

Flavia gave the Brigadier a peevish look. I could see why she was annoyed with him.

'Did I say the wrong thing?' he asked her.

'Yes.'

'Well, I've never pretended to be a bloody diplomat,' he replied with a sulky growl.

Quick as a flash, I mentally stripped away part of the mystery. The Brigadier had been in the castle all the time. But he had been deliberately kept out of my sight for fear he would spoil the plan of persuading me to give up the emeralds. No wonder Flavia had reckoned she could manage without him.

'It was unworthy of you, Flavia,' I said with quiet aplomb, 'to mislead me about your intentions for the emeralds. So I take it you are not on my side, after all?'

'You really are rather sweet, Oliver,' parried the girl. 'A sort of innocent abroad. But you have got it right now. We are not on your side.'

Who was? I seemed to be alone in this mysterious country, with a bewildering variety of enemies. It was all becoming far too complicated.

But there was one ray of light. It came from the small, hard object which pressed snugly against my ribs. The priceless Rassendyll ruby was still secreted on my person. Flavia would not dare to tell her unpleasant family that she had given it to me. Had she not said that her father would be violently angry at its loss? If I could only get the ruby to Lord Pargiter, this would be a feather in my cap. And I badly needed a few such feathers to counterbalance the unfortunate loss of the damned emeralds.

I felt the Brigadier's malevolent gaze boring into me.

'You may not be aware, my dear Mandrake,' he remarked, with a grim attempt at Club manners, 'that this castle has a complete set of fully working torture chambers. A most interesting survival of the Middle Ages, when we Elphbergs were by no means squeamish. The leather straps have been replaced, the pulleys are kept well oiled. It's one of Karl's duties. The State Tourist Bureau pays for the upkeep. It's an aspect of the Castle of Elphberg which seems to appeal particularly to our foreign visitors.'

'How bizarre,' I replied lightly. 'I don't think I've ever seen a torture chamber.'

'You will, Mandrake,' snapped the Brigadier. 'You will.'

I affected to take this as a piece of savage badinage. I did not want the brute to think I was frightened of him, though inwardly I was shaking like a jelly. It was obvious tactics for the Rassendylls to try to scare me, in the hope of learning more about the emeralds. But my delicate antennae, almost always so reliable, told me that, in the last instance, they were unlikely to use violence. After all, they had an established social position in England. They were not eccentric Continentals like Professor Lemberg or adventurers like Easingwold. I could make things very hot for them at home if they attempted to harm a senior member of the British Diplomatic Service. Brigadier Rudolph, though highly unprepossessing, was at least a gentleman. He was a fellow member of Black's with Sir Edmund Byfield. And he had been educated at Harrow and Brasenose. A posture of massive composure would be the best way to calm him. I had noticed before that this often worked with the upper echelons of the British Establishment.

Suddenly the butler Karl ran into the room and whispered urgently to his master, the Archduke.

'We must hurry,' said our host. 'The expected party of visitors are on their way up to the castle now by coach. It's the weekly Alberic Tour arriving early. And this time they include the whole British negotiating team from Strelsau. We have to treat them as V.I.P.s They will all need refreshments.'

It was gratifying to see the Rassendylls look distinctly rattled. I permitted myself a small, triumphant smirk. Real help was at hand at last.

It was unpleasantly hot behind the arras, in the space between the tapestries and the wall. It was not the ideal place to hide. I could not help remembering what had happened to poor Polonius. But the Rassendylls had been adamant. The tourists would be roaming all over the Castle. I must be kept right out of the way. To my chagrin and disappointment, Henry was stationed beside me with a revolver. He was to shoot me immediately if I tried to move or shout.

'You wouldn't dare to do that,' I commented. 'It would take a lot of explanation to your foreign visitors.'

'Don't be too sure,' said the Brigadier nastily. 'Guns have a habit of going off unexpectedly in this neck of the woods. It would be a sad accident. And you would be rather dead.'

I decided to take no risks. As a trained diplomatist and a

95

much loved only son and nephew, I am too valuable a commodity for the nation to lose. But it was hard to keep quiet when, through a chink in the loosely woven material, I saw the British delegation enter the great hall. That distinguished figure in a Savile Row pinstripe suit could only belong to Lord Pargiter. Beside him hopped the little runt, Trevor Flask. Not far away I recognized Joanna Tripp, a mature semi-virgin with whom I had once dallied when she occupied a prominent position in the Foreign Office typing pool. It is a small world in the higher reaches of diplomacy.

The British delegation seemed to have got temporarily separated from their Ruritanian hosts. I felt a wild urge to push the Rassendyll ruby through the chink in the tapestries. It would be a sensationally convenient way to deliver it to Lord Pargiter. It was almost as if he had come all this way to collect it. But even Trevor Flask's hawk-like intelligence might not at once realise what it was. And by the time he did, I might have a bullet in the brain.

'Where is the Professor?' asked Lord Pargiter.

'In the lavatory,' replied Flask.

'A most cultured fellow,' opined the British statesman. 'And quite a gentleman. We might offer him a visiting fellowship at All Souls. I'll talk to the Warden. Who was that funny old boy in the entrance hall? Is he the concierge?'

'That was the King of Ruritania.'

'Oh Lord, how awkward! Of course we were briefed. What on earth do I call him? Could I get away with Archduke?'

'Mr Elphberg would be more correct. The negotiations are going so well. We don't want a setback, Lord Pargiter.'

'A pity about that, Trevor. I'm an old monarchist at heart. But I defer to your expertise. We ought to get the King out to England though. It would be more decent. The Rassendylls would look after him. I'll talk to Brigadier Rudy some day at Black's.'

'The King wouldn't want to leave,' said Trevor.

'Why on earth not?'

'His home is here.'

'Aren't people extraordinary? But I respect your insights. Ah, my dear Professor! Do come and tell us about these wonderful tapestries.'

I craned my neck to look at the Professor. It was none other than my old enemy, the unspeakable Amadeus Lemberg. Once again a thrill of horror shot through my veins. I could never forget now his connection with State security. Perhaps he had really come to Elphberg to search for me? It was an appalling thought.

Lemberg gave a prolonged dissertation on the tapestries in his old pedantic manner, explaining their historical connection with the great wall hangings in the Wawel Castle at Cracow in Poland. I no longer found him so charming.

'You are a mine of information, Professor,' said Lord Pargiter with almost royal graciousness. 'We are favoured to have you with us. But I thought you had a full time job at Zenda.'

'I do indeed,' said Amadeus, with a tinge of justifiable awkwardness. 'And an important one too, if I may say so. But I have very recently been posted to Strelsau on a temporary assignment. That's why the Ministry chose me to join you.'

I was glad the old charlatan had indeed lost his cushy billet at Zenda. No doubt my escape had been ill-received at headquarters. But it would not have endeared me to him. I hoped we should not meet again.

'When you were at Zenda,' said Flask, 'did you ever encounter an old colleague of mine? His name is Oliver Mandrake. He has been staying on holiday at the Zenda Palace.'

'Mandrake?' replied Lemberg casually. 'I'm not sure I remember the name.'

'You couldn't miss him,' continued Flask. 'He is plump and unathletic and a bit of a gossip. Fancies himself with the girls.'

'He certainly does,' commented Joanna Tripp drily. She was standing almost in front of me. I longed to give her a kick.

'I do recall your friend now,' said Lemberg with little enthusiasm. 'He came to one of our concerts at the Castle. But he left the hotel shortly afterwards. They said he ran up quite a bill at the bar.'

'Sounds the same man,' sniggered Flask.

I fumed inwardly. Was there to be no end to this character-assassination? I longed to machine-gun the whole bunch. Nor did I care for the stifled grin on the face of Henry Rassendyll.

'It is always a pleasure to meet our British friends,' continued the Professor smoothly. 'You take such a keen interest in our artistic treasures. These lovely tapestries for example.'

'Oh, Mr Flask is a complete barbarian,' said Lord Pargiter. 'He only comes on these cultural trips to prevent me from making diplomatic blunders.'

Was there tension between the two, as I sincerely hoped? Or was Pargiter sufficiently fond of Flask to feel able to tease him in public?

'Mr Flask may be more interested in the historical aspect of the Castle.' said Lemberg in his usual ingratiating manner. 'Of course the story of King Alberic is more legend than fact, like that of his Transylvanian contemporary Dracul. But his activities were undoubtedly macabre.'

'I'm told there are dungeons here,' commented Lord Pargiter hopefully.

'Certainly. And you shall see them. It's part of the standard tour. An outstanding feature is the rack, still in working order. People used to get their arms and legs stretched on it in a most cruel way. It was one of the most effective forms of torture.'

'Well, I'm against that,' said Lord Pargiter pensively. 'But I suppose it had its uses in the primitive socio-economic conditions of the time. The State needed information. It's all a question of the relative balance between the rights of the individual and those of the community. After all, they hadn't read Rousseau then, though they did know a little Aristotle. I might do a piece on that theme for one of the better weeklies.'

'I think Alberic tormented his victims more for fun,' said the Professor. 'There is an evil streak in the Elphberg genetic line.'

'I'd love to see the rack,' put in Joanna Tripp. 'Then I could mention it in one of my letters home to Auntie.'

'But certainly, dear lady,' said Lemberg, with old-world gallantry. 'Allow me to escort you personally to the torture chamber.'

Pargiter and Flask were left briefly together. It should have been my moment. But young Henry was watching me like a hawk.

'He said one interesting thing,' whispered Flask. 'Mandrake has left Zenda.'

'But he was told to wait there for instructions.'

'Exactly, Lord Pargiter. He must have disobeyed.'

'How very strange.'

'Not to those who know him. Mandrake is a perfect ass.

98

He's capable of almost any aberration.'

'Does that matter?'

'It could. His part in our scheme of things is only small. But Mandrake has an extraordinary talent for causing trouble. I tried not to use him here but I was overruled. We don't want him lousing up the Grand Design.'

'Don't bother me with minutiae, dear boy.' said Pargiter with aristocratic disdain. 'I am interested in the body politic. Your friend is a mere pimple on that great body.'

'Mandrake may be a pimple,' retorted the irrepressible Flask. 'But a pimple on the bottom can be damned troublesome.'

Henry was smirking as they left the hall and his tension relaxed. I felt exceedingly hurt and cross. It was really abominable that my professional colleagues should refer to me in so cavalier a manner. And it was strange and sinister that, believing themselves alone, they should so offensively minimize my role in the whole affair. After all, I was the bearer of the Elphberg emeralds. At least I would have been, if I had not lost them. Mine was no small responsibility. As a senior diplomatist of considerable experience, it was intolerable to hear oneself described to a member of the Upper House as a pimple on the posterior.

It seemed an age before the Brigadier burst into the great hall. Flavia followed him.

'You can come out now,' he shouted. 'Your friends have gone.'

My friends had gone! And, with them, all hope of rescue. I felt definitely mouldy.

'Cheer up, Mandrake,' said the Brigadier with rough humour. 'I like men of guts.'

'I have plenty of guts,' I snapped, though inwardly quaking. 'In fact, crisis rather excites me. I have always enjoyed tough assignments. I like to be fully stretched.'

The Brigadier burst into demonic laughter.

'Fully stretched!' he shrieked. 'That's really rather apt. Fully stretched is just what you will be, my dear Mandrake, when Karl and I get you on that rack.'

'When is that to be?' asked Henry enthusiastically.

'Here and now. No time like the present. We need to get the secret out of him.'

99

'I know nothing,' I shrieked. 'I've lost the bloody emeralds. I can't help you.'

'It will be getting dark down there now,' said Flavia calmly. 'Candles are so cumbrous. Why don't you wait till the morning?'

'It shouldn't take long,' replied the Brigadier. 'A few turns and he'll tell all.'

'I'll make us all some of my nice peppered stew,' said Flavia. 'And then Cousin Michael and I will play the Kreutzer sonata.'

'Oh, all right,' agreed the Brigadier peevishly. 'But Mandrake and I have a rendezvous at dawn.'

When he had gone, I turned to Flavia.

'Thank you,' I said simply.

'I didn't want the dinner to be late.' she replied.

I did not expect to enjoy dinner.

'I wish you'd persuade your father to give me the benefit of the doubt,' I said plaintively. 'My tolerance of pain is not high.'

Henry and his sister looked at each other in surprise. Then they both laughed.

'You've got it wrong.' said Henry.

'The man who has just left this room,' added Flavia, 'is not our father. We have only just realized that you were under that misunderstanding. Our father is Brigadier Rudolph Rassendyll.'

'I know. I met him in Sussex. Then who is this man here?'

'His twin brother. Uncle Rupert. Another traditional family name. He is the Earl of Burlesdon.'

'Lord Burlesdon! But I thought he was – in seclusion.'

'You thought he was mad and locked away.' said Henry.

'Well, he is really.' added Flavia.

'Why is he here then?' I asked.

'I suppose it's our fault. But you see, Uncle Rupert has never actually killed anyone. Though there have been some awkward little episodes. He has a trace of the Alberic streak.'

'So I noticed.'

'His seclusion is voluntary,' continued Flavia. 'So I'm allowed to take him out for little holidays every so often. This year he is supposed to be at Bognor Regis. But we took a chance and brought him here instead.'

'That was most irresponsible of you,' I said.

'I suppose it was a bit naughty.' replied Flavia. 'But Uncle Rupert is so sweet when he's on good form. He loves birds and mountain flowers.'

'I have yet to see that side of him,' I replied frostily.

'Uncle Rupert really has taken command of the Castle this year,' said Henry. 'Karl and the men are scared stiff of him. His word is law.'

'We shall just have to humour him,' agreed Flavia comfortably. 'Poor old Oliver! It will mean a night in the dungeons, I'm afraid. That's where Uncle Rupert will expect to find you. When he comes with the men at dawn.'

I shuddered. The girl's revelation had appalled me. It would have been bad enough to find oneself the prisoner of a quarrelsome senior officer of peppery disposition and ferocious demeanour, as I knew the Brigadier to be. But I had been able to comfort myself with the delusion that he was unlikely to resort to physical violence. Now I knew that my actual situation was much more serious. I was at the mercy of a dangerous lunatic of sadistic tastes, incorrectly removed quite recently from an asylum. Lord Burlesdon was demented and would stick at nothing. The prospect was uninviting in the extreme. Once again I passed a restless night. I was losing a lot of sleep on this Ruritanian assignment.

'Don't scream, Oliver.'

'Who is it?'

'It's me. Flavia. I've come to let you out.'

'I thought I was due to be tortured.'

'You were. That's why I'm helping you to escape. Uncle Rupert is not reliable.'

'I'm glad you've realized that in time.'

'Rupert and Henry will be furious when they find you've gone. You'd better give them a wide berth.'

'I certainly will. What time is it?'

'Half an hour before dawn.'

'Just in time, thank God. Flavia, you're a marvellous girl. But will I be safe?'

'There will be hazards on the hillside. To begin with,

nobody here must suspect that I have helped you. So you will have to climb down outside the window. The first light will help you.'

'It looks a long way down.'

'It is. That's why I have tied your sheets into a rope ladder. I hope it reaches far enough.'

'It isn't quite my style.'

'The others may not spot that. I told them last night that you were a past President of the Oxford University Mountaineering Club.'

'There may be beasts at the bottom.'

'Our dogs are shut up. And wolves seldom attack a grown man in daylight. Just keep on going downhill. Eventually you will find a road. You should be able to get a lift into Strelsau.'

'But everyone's looking for me there.'

'Take this paper. An address is written on it. You can't miss it. It's in the principal street, the old Königstrasse.'

'Who lives there, Flavia?'

'A reliable Ruritanian person who used to live near me in London. We are on friendly terms. They will help you.'

'I'm eternally grateful. But why are you doing all this for me?'

'Well, I suppose I've got a bit of a soft spot for you, after all. You are such a deliciously helpless old booby. And I didn't want the mad Earl to do something rather shattering to you. England is my home. We have a certain position to maintain there. You will co-operate over that, won't you? You won't tell people that the Rassendylls are peculiar?'

'Nothing was further from my thoughts.'

'Daddy, the sane Brigadier, is hoping to become Lord Lieutenant of the county. It would mean invitations to Buckingham Palace and other lovely things. You won't shatter his dream, will you?'

'On condition that you get Lord Burlesdon back under lock and key as soon as possible.'

'I knew you would help us, Oliver dear. You are a sweet man and a valuable member of the Establishment. It's good to work with you. We are royal but we're not awfully normal. Do you think you could get Henry into the Foreign Office?'

'I rather doubt it.'

'He's got such beautiful manners, hasn't he? Perhaps he'd

102

be better in the British Council. He likes working with foreigners.'

'I'd like to get going. There are creaking noises somewhere near here. They may be oiling the pulleys.'

'I hope I can rely on you, Oliver. It would be a shame if Daddy lost his ticket for the Royal Enclosure at Ascot. You see nothing strange in the Rassendylls?'

'The family is robustly normal.'

'You're a poppet, Oliver. And you've got the Rassendyll ruby safe?'

'Sure.'

'I want you to take it. It will buy your silence. And it will make life easier for Cousin Michael.'

'You're glorious.'

'Whistle softly when you get to the bottom. If you do.'

Some hours later I awoke in the bushes from a sleep of profound exhaustion. It had been a ghastly run down the hillside. My ankles felt exceedingly painful. Nor could I dismiss the horrid fear that the Rassendylls might set their dogs to follow my scent, even though I had crossed more than one stream. Eventually I had just collapsed in the undergrowth. Now the road curled below me. The sinister Castle of Elphberg could be seen only in the dim distance, an emblem of Gothic horror high up on the edge of the snow-capped mountains. At last, for the first time for some days, I was free and alone. The only depressing aspects were that I had lost the emeralds and that three separate groups of ruthless enemies were combing the country to find me. But once in Strelsau I could report to Lord Pargiter and it would then be his responsibility to solve my problems.

Suddenly I saw a large bus coming down the road. Scrambling up with an effort, I waved my arms. It stopped and I was summoned aboard.

'Oh look, Bess,' said a decidedly North American female voice, 'there's a quaint native.'

'He looks awfully dirty. I'll bet he's got a pong. Motion to him to sit at the back.'

'Do be careful, Muriel. Some of these natives understand English.'

'This one won't, dear. He's definitely primitive. I'm not sure he's all there.'

'He could be a gypsy. Perhaps he plays the violin. We shall be stopping for lunch in a vineyard. There's going to be folk-dancing. We'll get him going then.'

The thought of folk-dancing filled me with horror. I still felt decidedly below par. But at least I was camouflaged by the foreign group and was making progress away from the Castle of Elphberg. I had forgotten how bizarre my appearance must seem after my sufferings over the last few days. At least it was a way of travelling incognito. Nobody would have recognized in me now the well-groomed, senior diplomatist who had disappeared so mysteriously from the Castle of Zenda and was now being hunted throughout the land.

'My, oh my, Bess,' continued a voice which sounded not unlike a circular saw in motion, 'I sure have enjoyed this trip. There will be so much to tell the folks back in Toronto. Grandmother was from Strelsau, you know. It's been just swell for me to renew tactile contact with my Ruritanian heritage. They are a handsome race, aren't they? Take that poor man in the back. His cheek bones are just typically Ruritanian.'

'I think he's a mess.'

'Of course he's a mess. But he'd clean up real pretty. He reminds me a bit of my Elmer.'

'Look at his hands, Muriel. They're filthy but they're soft. He's never done hard work.'

'Probably a scrounger. Elmer always said that socialism fosters scroungers. He was a believer in the Protestant work ethic.'

'He's staring at us in such a funny way.'

'How could Elmer be staring at us, dear? It's five years since he went over Niagara Falls.'

'I mean the man at the back. I do hope he doesn't follow our drift.'

'Probably just a loony. There's a lot of inbreeding in these parts. You can tell he's a bit daft from the shape of his head.'

'I hope he won't stick to us when we get to Strelsau this evening.'

'No danger of that, darling. We're not such delectable chicks any more.'

'Speak for yourself, Bess. My masseuse says I've still got good, firm Canadian flesh. I'm just longing for a nice soap-down in a hot bath at the Hilton.'

I had gained one useful nugget of information. The bus was due in Strelsau that evening. I was on the right road. In my relief, I favoured Bess and Muriel with one of my more charismatic smiles.

'He just grinned at us, Muriel. It was sort of touching. He must have a kind heart.'

'He's got a lot of tartar on the teeth. I wish we could offer him a good clean-up. Those bathrooms are big enough for two.'

'Really, darling, you do say the strangest things. You're not supposed to bath the natives. It goes against their national pride.'

It seemed to be tacitly accepted that I would join the Canadian ladies for a much needed lunch at one of the State wine farms. I felt like Caliban with a brace of mature Mirandas. The subsequent demonstration by a folk-dancing troupe became rather wearisome. Afterwards they encouraged the visitors to join in the dancing.

'Do you think I might cavort with our friend here?' asked Bess.

'He might have lice. Or nits in the hair.'

'I'll take the risk. If only he wasn't so filthy, he could be quite gorgeous.'

Bess whirled and stamped until I felt quite enveloped in her firm, Canadian flesh. I was glad to relapse into torpor when we had boarded the bus again.

'Did he dance well, Bess?' asked Muriel.

'He had potential. I could feel it, darling.'

At last we were gliding through the suburbs of Strelsau. The guidebooks were right about its being a picturesque city. Under Elphberg rule there had not been enough money around to finance the replacement of ancient buildings. The most beautiful cities of Europe are those which had the good fortune to be poor during the nineteenth and twentieth centuries. Even the so-called new city of Strelsau was old, like the new towns of Edinburgh and Warsaw. The architecture was eighteenth-century baroque. The old city itself was genuinely mediaeval. In its heart stood the Strelsau Hilton, at the entrance to the Königstrasse, now called the Vlpszt.

'How do we get rid of the native?' asked Muriel.

'Just give him a cheery wave. He'll get the message.'

'It's a shame we can't clean him up. I'll bet he strips well.'

'Really, dear, you're getting quite shameless.'

The opportunity was too good to miss. I threw security to the winds.

'Thank you, ladies, for a most enjoyable journey,' I said with massive dignity.

As the swing door of the Strelsau Hilton revolved them out of sight, it was delightful to see the surprise and consternation registered on the good-humoured faces of the matrons from Toronto.

I was on my own again. And this time I was in the heart of the capital city. It was a most dangerous place for me to walk around in during the hours of daylight. My appearance was weird. I had no identification papers and spoke not a word of the local language. The State security police would be looking for me everywhere. At all costs I must get quickly to the refuge which Flavia had arranged for me. It was my only hope.

Fortunately I had no great difficulty in locating the address which I had been given. It turned out to be a large and elderly apartment block on the main boulevard, between the cathedral and the opera house. The main door stood open and you could just walk up to the right floor for the flat you wanted. I did so and rang the bell.

The door opened quickly. A substantial figure stood in the dark entrance.

'Come in, Oliver Mandrake,' said a not unfamiliar voice. 'I was expecting you.'

'You were expecting me?' I asked, in faltering tones. Something seemed very wrong.

'Flavia telephoned to tell me you were on your way.'

A whiskered face was thrust forward. I nearly fainted in horror. I was looking into the dark, piercing eyes of Dr Gertrude Markovitz.

106

'You won't betray me?' I asked anxiously. 'You really are on my side?'

The mellow bass-baritone of Dr Gertrude sounded comfortingly aunt-like through the evening gloom.

'Yes, Oliver,' she said. 'I am on your side.'

A hot bath, a huge whisky and a substantial dinner had done wonders for my morale. My hostess's assurances of help had also been most welcome.

'That wasn't your attitude in the Castle of Zenda,' I probed. 'You were prepared to do unspeakable things to key portions of my anatomy.'

'Don't be harsh to me, Oliver dear. You must try to understand. Poor Amadeus is an old friend. I had to help him when he was in trouble with State Security. He was desperate to get the emeralds back. But now the situation has changed. I accept your word that you don't know where they are. So I can afford to divulge my real feelings for you. These are warmly friendly.'

I shuddered mentally. This grotesque person had clearly fallen victim to my fatal charm. But perhaps that was just as well. Otherwise she might have delivered me to my enemies. As it was, she seemed to be prepared to cherish me. And how I needed cherishing, after the appalling hardships and dangers I had already suffered in this unpredictable country.

'How did Flavia know we knew each other?' I asked.

'She didn't. It was pure coincidence. You see, for a time we lived almost next door to each other in Hampstead. She became interested in me when she heard where I came from. We were quite good friends. But I haven't met her family.'

'You are lucky,' I said crisply.

'I don't know anything about their politics or plots,' continued Gertrude. 'Of course they are considered highly controversial here. I just think of Flavia as an attractive young friend.'

'It was fortunate she put us in touch again.'

'The hand of Fate, my dear Oliver.'

'But won't you run a great risk by shielding me here?' I asked. 'The whole apparatus of the State will be after me. It will be a black mark against you if I am found here.'

'I am prepared to risk that.'

'I don't quite understand your motive.'

'My dear boy, you are too modest. You have a certain charm. Even your figure is rather sweet. And I'm a lonely woman who needs a friend.'

'It's more than that.'

'Yes, you're quite right. The truth is, Oliver, that I find you professionally rather stimulating.'

'I don't quite understand.'

'You know about my specialization in sex therapy. I am achieving spectacular results in that field. And I feel sure I can help you.'

'But I don't need help. At least,' I added hastily 'not in that area.'

'My poor Oliver, you must be frank with me. We have discussed all this before at Zenda.'

'I remember only too well.'

'The first hurdle is to recognize your problem quite honestly. You're a well-developed man in the prime of life. And yet your response to women is far from satisfactory.'

'You're barking up the wrong tree, Gertude. I adore women. I think about them all the time. Even now, when I've had a sort of aversion therapy treatment. I have certainly met some appalling females in Ruritania.'

I could not help remembering my gruesome encounters with Barbara Canterbury-Cooper and Flavia Rassendyll, not to mention Gertrude herself.

'That's not very gallant, Oliver. It's symptomatic of your attitude. There is certainly something inadequate in your response to me so far.'

It was on the tip of my tongue to tell this tiresome woman that I simply did not find her attractive. But nothing would have infuriated her more. And I could not afford to do that. She was my only hope.

'We will have a session in my laboratory before bedtime,' said Gertrude. 'Don't look so nervous, dear. Most patients find it all rather fun.'

'So you're looking forward to experimenting on me?'

'I certainly am, Oliver. So long as you respond positively to my course of treatment, you will be a welcome and safe guest in my little apartment.'

The blackmail was only too apparent. I should be protected

so long as I submitted to the ministrations of this voraciously sex-obsessed old harridan. But any sign of resistance would cause me to be handed over to my enemies. Betrayal would lurk always round the corner. It was an appalling predicament. My situation would be little more enviable than it had been in the hateful castles of Zenda, Tarlenheim and Elphberg. The woman's physical rapacity might prove too much for my diminished physique. She seemed a veritable harpy. But I had absolutely no alternative. The immediate requirement was to produce some show of enthusiasm. I only hoped I could manage it.

'Do you agree to my terms?' asked Gertrude sharply.

'Yes.' I replied heavily. 'I agree to your terms. Perhaps you can help me too in other ways. Ruritanian politics have become frightfully confusing.'

'Poor dear boy, it's all been too much for you. Let me ruffle your hair a bit.'

'I used to like those Wild West films where they had goodies and baddies. The goodies were white and the baddies brown. Then they became racially conscious. So after that the goodies were brown and the baddies white. But at least there was a clear distinction. You knew where you were. Ruritania is not like that at all. I never know who is on my side.'

'It's perfectly simple, dear. From all you told me when you were having your bath, your difficulties should not be exaggerated. You have only three sets of enemies. The State of Ruritania in the person of Professor Lemberg. The extreme Left personified by Gabriel Easingwold. And the House of Elphberg-Rassendyll led by the unhinged Earl of Burlesdon. Each group cherishes the illusion that you hold the key to the location of the crown jewels. All are prepared to torture or terrorize you until you tell them what they want to find out. All are searching actively for you for this declared purpose. That's all you need to know.'

'Thank you, Gertrude. A most lucid explanation. I feel quite cheerful now. Apart from torture and death, I have little to fear.'

'Once you start on my sex therapy course, you will think of little else. It will be a most relaxing way to pass the time.'

'But I have vital work to do, Gertrude. I must report my presence in Strelsau to Lord Pargiter. They will be worrying about me. The Foreign Office regard me as a key figure.'

'I should advise you to keep away from the British delegation for the time being. What they want from you are the emeralds. If you turn up without them, they might be rather unwelcoming.'

She was right. I could just imagine Flask's withering glances as I confessed my loss.

'I want the Elphberg emeralds!' I shouted. 'Where the Hell have they got to?'

'Keep calm, Oliver. Your faithful Gertrude has a bright idea. Why don't you advertise for the jewels?'

'Advertise? You must be mad.'

'In code of course.'

'But I haven't arranged a code with anyone else.'

'Really, Oliver, I'm beginning to wonder whether you are quite suited to this kind of work. All you have to do is to insert a notice in tomorrow's newspapers. In Ruritanian of course. I'll do it for you. I can ring through tonight. Just say that you want to buy a copy of Pollard's book, *Reptiles of Ruritania*. That might bring an answer. Whoever took the jewels out of that book might be ready to sell them back.'

'That's brilliant, Gertrude. But we mustn't give the address. I don't want the baddies turning up here.'

'I will just put a telephone number. And not the one listed in the book. I have a special, extra line for private patients.'

'You think of everything. But suppose some of those awful people see the advertisement? It could lead them in my direction. I have a horror of that.'

'You must take a certain risk, Oliver. It's better than being caught like a rat in a trap. It would be no bad thing for you to act as a decoy.'

'A decoy?' I almost shrieked.

'Why, yes. You need your enemies to come out in the open. Especially as you are safely tucked away here. My advertisement could lead to movement.'

'I don't doubt that. I only hope it's the right kind of movement.'

'Poor Oliver, always so afraid. You need a woman to inspire you. I'll go and telephone the newspapers. You can watch the news on television. When I come back, we'll adjourn to the laboratory.'

110

'So late at night?'

'That's the nicest time.'

The news in Ruritania lacked interest for me. But I stiffened to attention when the fleshy features of Lord Pargiter appeared on the screen. The vulture-like countenance of Trevor Flask came shortly afterwards. It was some satisfaction to see that he was beginning to grow bald on top. My own hair is glossy and profuse. The British delegation appeared to be attending a banquet at the Strelsau Hilton. There were speeches and champagne. I could distinctly see old Pargiter swilling it down.

Tears of chagrin welled into my eyes as I thought of the contrast between their situation and my own. Just down the road, my colleagues were whooping it up at the expense of the Ruritanian taxpayer, enjoying the good things of life on which I am no mean expert. Whereas I myself, pursued by fiends from Hell, was cooped up with an eccentric sex-therapist of unpleasing appearance. It really was too bad. And what had my colleagues done for me? Nothing at all, except to make snide remarks about my embonpoint.

Well, I would get my revenge. The sniggering would cease abruptly when I appeared with the emeralds.

I felt sure somehow that Gertrude's advertisement would produce a reply. But whose would be the mysterious voice that breathed down the telephone on the private line? The thought of myself as a human decoy was far from pleasing.

When the telephone did indeed ring next day, I nearly jumped out of my skin.

'Don't answer it,' I shrieked in sudden panic.

'Shut up, you silly boy,' snapped Gertrude. 'This could be the end of the beginning.'

'More likely,' I moaned, 'the beginning of the end.'

My hostess gabbled away in Ruritanian. Then she put down the receiver with a smile of satisfaction. I could see that there was something afoot and my heart sank.

'You're in luck, Oliver,' she said. 'We're in action again.'

'Horrors!' I hissed.

'That was a message. For the advertiser who wishes to buy Pollard, *Reptiles of Ruritania*. A seller is interested. You are to

111

meet this evening at six o'clock. But you must come alone. That is an essential condition.'

A thrill of horror ran through me.

'I won't go anywhere dark or lonely,' I said hastily. 'I've had enough of all that.'

'There will be no need for that,' explained Gertrude calmly. 'All you have to do is to attend the evening Mass in the cathedral. Sit in the third row on the lefthand side.'

'What will happen then?'

'I have no idea. Presumably the person who answered the advertisement will contact you.'

'I hope to God it isn't Easingwold. It isn't a face I shall easily forget. What did the voice sound like?'

'It was a Ruritanian. Could have been a light man's voice or a deep woman's. Of course anyone could have paid a hotel porter to put through a call. Your contact could be a foreigner. Even an Englishman.'

'Not Lord Burlesdon!' I almost shrieked, remembering his manic eyes.

'You'll just have to wait and see, dear.'

'I hope I shall be safe.'

'There is obviously an element of risk. But you do want the emeralds back, don't you?'

'I suppose so,' I answered doubtfully.

'Brace up, Oliver. Be a man. I shall be there to protect you.'

'But I am supposed to go alone.'

'I don't care for the sound of that. It could be a trap. All the more reason why I should be hovering unobtrusively in the background.'

'Is that quite your line, Gertrude dear?'

'Well, the cathedral is not my usual stamping ground. But I shall find somewhere to perch.'

'I appreciate that. You're a loyal soul.'

'Don't stare round, looking for me, Oliver. That would give the game away. You will be able to recognize me from my feet. I shall be wearing my blue socks and embroidered slippers. Make for them in an emergency.'

'You think there may be one?'

'One can't be too careful. We are dealing with ruthless killers.'

'I find you so comforting, my dear Gertrude. But at least it

112

isn't far from here. Is it a fine old church?'

'I suppose so. It's dedicated to the Archangel Michael. In the eastern branch of the Christian church, Saint Michael has a special significance.'

'And what is that?' I asked breezily.

'He is the Angel of Death.'

I felt too nervous to do much solid praying in the cathedral that evening. The church was huge and dark, and cool in spite of the summer weather. The worshippers, though not numerous, seemed to have crowded into the first few benches. I felt surrounded on all sides by well-muffled elderly people. Any of them could have been my contact. It was impossible to see faces in the gloom. The Mass proceeded at leisurely pace. I longed to get the ordeal over with and be out again in the fresh night air.

And where was Gertrude? The woman was a good sport and my feelings towards her were now quite kindly. At least she had given me shelter in the hour of crisis. It would be comforting to feel assured of her presence. But there was not a pair of blue socks to be seen.

Suddenly I spotted her. I gave the old girl full marks for ingenuity. Not far away on my left was a large, ornamental box for confessions. It was not at present in use. The place for the priest in the middle was vacant, and the light to show that confessions were being heard was naturally not turned on. On each side of the priest's compartment, there was a place for one penitent. The upper part of the box was screened in with wood, but not the lower part. This was to show whether the box was empty or not. I saw now that one of the boxes was in fact occupied. This was hardly surprising. Some zealous penitent was perhaps anxious to be first when the confessions started. The legs of a kneeling woman protruded from the box. And they ended in blue socks and embroidered slippers. Clever Gertrude must have been planning this all along. She had chosen the one place in the cathedral where she could be close at hand without being seen.

Now my attention was diverted again to the Mass. We had reached the part where the kiss of peace is given. Under the

113

modern rites, the congregation are encouraged to participate enthusiastically in this process. I was not therefore greatly surprised when a muffled figure on my right, of indeterminate age and sex, turned towards me and hugged me warmly in its arms. Balkan Christianity is bound to be a bit extravagant compared with our more decorous practices at Sevenoaks.

But the outcome was distinctly unusual. I found myself holding a small, well-wrapped package. It must have been thrust into my hands under cover of the kiss of peace. I turned to ask some of the obvious questions. But the figure on my right had disappeared.

What was I to do? The package might contain anything, even a bomb. Clearly I was supposed to secrete it about my person. But suppose it blew up, and I with it? I felt badly the need for urgent advice. What more natural than that I should turn towards the confessional? After all, I was in the middle of a course of therapy in the skilled hands of Dr Markovitz. She, my wise woman, would tell me what to do.

Now I saw that there was something different about the confessional since I had last looked. A priest had entered the central section. The wooden partition at the top of his box had been closed in the usual way and you could not see his face. But his legs and feet could be seen, showing that his compartment was occupied. These were facing me directly, whereas Gertrude's were in profile.

How awkward for her, I thought with amusement. She must have been caught unawares and would now have to make her confession. It would be a new experience for her but no doubt she would have plenty of material.

But there was something badly wrong. My quick perception signalled to my trained brain a message of desperate warning. The priest's black boots! Priests did not wear boots like that, at least not in church on a summer evening. Who did then? Soldiers and policemen. And then I noticed with horror that Gertrude's feet were strangely still, as if frozen in the very act of receiving absolution.

I dashed to the confessional box and thrust aside the flimsy screen which concealed her face. My only thought was to rush us both out of the cathedral as quickly as possible. At first I thought Gertrude had fainted. She was hunched up in the chair, leaning against the wire mesh which separated her compartment from that of the priest. Beyond the mesh, on the other side, was a small wooden hatch which must have been shut by the occupant of the priest's box. Then I noticed a small gash in Gertrude's forehead. It did not seem to have made much of a wound. I thought she might have grazed her head while falling forward. But was she breathing? I could hear no sound. And her pulse seemed to have no movement. Suddenly the sickening truth flashed into my fevered brain. Gertrude was dead. She had been murdered.

To this day I do not remember how I got out of that cathedral. But I know I moved fast. At all costs I did not want to come face to face with the man in the black boots. I was in intense danger of doing so while I remained in the confessional with the body of poor Gertrude. At any moment her murderer might slide back the wooden panel again and stare me in the eyes. It was an appalling thought.

There was also the danger that people in the congregation would soon spot what had happened to Gertrude. My presence in her vicinity might have been noted. If so, I could be held as a possible murderer.

Palpitating with horror and shock, I dashed down the Königstrasse to the comparative, if deceptive, safety of Gertrude's apartment. It seemed lonely without her. I had developed a soft spot for the friendly old thing. Even her ministrations in the cause of sex therapy had not been entirely unpleasing. I had grown accustomed to her face, and even her moustache.

But why had she been killed? Was the murderer working in concert with the person who had passed me the parcel? Or did the two represent quite separate forces, one perhaps benevolent and the other malevolent, a good and a bad fairy? It was all most confusing.

Only now did I remember that I still had in my pocket the small packet given me in the cathedral. With trembling fingers I tore open the paper and slid off the string. Then I gasped. Lying on my knees were the Elphberg emeralds. How gloriously they gleamed, these doomed gems for which I had been threatened with torture and death.

With computer-like precision, my keen mind told me that this development totally changed my position. I already held the Rassendyll ruby which Flavia had given me at the Castle of Elphberg. Now it was simply a question of handing the ruby and the emeralds over to Lord Pargiter. He would deal with them after that. It would also be his job to get me safely out of the country. He could, for example, add me to his official delegation and thus protect me with the cloak of diplomatic immunity. Protection was exactly what I most needed. But I must have equal status with Trevor Flask. Even Trevor would be obliged to give me a hero's welcome. With verve and dash, I had got the emeralds through to Strelsau.

Picking up Gertrude's telephone, I dialled the number of the Strelsau Hilton. Of course they spoke English on the switchboard. I asked to be put through to Lord Pargiter's suite. Eventually the substandard vowels of Trevor Flask came on the line.

'Lord Pargiter is a little busy just now. Can I help you? Who is that speaking?'

'Oliver Mandrake. I'm in Strelsau.'

'Oh, Christ!'

'Trevor, I've got sensational news. I must see you at once. The most appalling things have been happening to me.'

'Cool it, Oliver. Be careful what you say on the phone.'

'I want to see Lord Pargiter. Here and now.'

'He's off duty.'

'It's a matter of life or death.'

'The truth is, Oliver, that it's Joanna's birthday. You'll remember her. Lord Pargiter is standing drinks for the occasion. He's frightfully good with junior staff.'

'If you've got a cake,' I said tartly, 'it won't be easy to find room for all those candles.'

'That was a bit bitchy, Oliver. You seem to be on form. Well, come and see us in the morning.'

'No, no. It must be tonight. I'm in the most ghastly danger.'

'If you insist, you can join us for dinner. A group of us are going out to the Gay Musketeer in half an hour. It's a folklore place with a gypsy band.'

'Not somewhere dubious, I hope? We bachelors have our reputations to sustain.'

116

'The adjective is used in the old-fashioned sense. All the taxi drivers know it.'

'I'll be there.'

'It's a party, Oliver. Lord Pargiter will want to relax.'

'So do I, Trevor. I'm at the end of my tether.'

The gypsy band at the Gay Musketeer fiddled away with extravagant enthusiasm. Speech was only just possible.

'This is Oliver Mandrake, Lord Pargiter,' said Trevor Flask with unctuous relish.

The statesman turned weary eyes towards me, as if I were something nasty the cat had brought in from the shrubbery.

'I have heard of you,' he announced with infinite resignation.

I flashed him one of my beaming smiles and composed my manly features into an expression of alert intelligence. Long experience of charming Top People has taught me the importance of first impressions.

'You've lost weight, Oliver,' said Joanna in an attempt at sprightly wit. 'And you were always such a snappy dresser.'

'I have been through the most appalling experiences,' I retorted. 'Death Row rather than Savile Row. No wonder I don't look exactly spruce.'

'I thought you were supposed to await our summons to Strelsau,' commented Lord Pargiter.

'Yes, indeed,' added the rat-like Flask. 'We don't understand why you left Zenda.'

'I can explain all,' I said hastily.

'Don't try too hard,' snapped the statesman, with an air of aristocratic hauteur which I found far from encouraging.

I was compelled to raise my voice in order to be heard above the Levantine wailing of the violins.

'It was not my fault that I had to leave the Zenda Palace,' I bawled. 'I was abducted. Since then I have been threatened with abdominal surgery, death by burning and torture on a mediaeval rack. A woman has been murdered under my very eyes. Three different terrorist groups are hot on my trail. I can't take much more. You've got to help me.'

Joanna Tripp burst into a peal of girlish laughter.

'Dear old Oliver!' she cackled. 'Just the same as ever.'

I flashed the forward hussy one of my coldest glares.

'Stop yelling, Oliver,' said Trevor Flask. 'Do you want to advertise your presence? You seem to have made an awful mess of things.'

'I resent that implication,' I retorted hotly.

'Oh, I don't know,' commented Lord Pargiter with a twitch of amusement. 'Mr Mandrake has rather enlivened our evening. It's so dull when everything goes smoothly. That's my only complaint about you, my dear Trevor.'

I gave Lord Pargiter a grateful glance. At least he had the sense to see that, unlike Flask, I possessed a certain entertainment value. The old politician and I were basically men of the same type, urbane, civilized and disillusioned. I must trade on that. The capricious Pargiter represented my only hope of escaping from the ghastly groups of enemies who were clearly now closing in on me from all sides.

'Where were you at school, Mandrake?' asked the delegation leader.

'Buntingford actually, Lord Pargiter. But I had an uncle at Rugby.'

'We had a beak at Eton who'd been to your place,' commented Lord Pargiter, almost with approval.

My danger was deadly. But these English rituals had to be played out. At least it was satisfactory to see the chagrin on Trevor's face. Educational badinage was one of the numerous topics he detested.

'And then of course I went up to Oxford,' I added. 'Balliol College.'

'Head of the River in my day,' commented Lord Pargiter nostalgically. 'But we bumped you once.'

Trevor's scowl was now horrible to behold.

'You had no right to leave Zenda without permission, Oliver,' he hissed. 'If people are really after you, it could be most compromising for us to be seen with you.'

'I didn't ask to come here,' I snapped.

'I think it's lovely to have Oliver with us on my birthday,' remarked the egotistical Joanna. 'He has life enhancing qualities.'

'His scholar gypsy appearance certainly adds an amusing

118

note of eccentricity,' said Lord Pargiter. 'That is something we have missed in our rather sober negotiations.'

'Mandrake at the negotiations,' groaned Flask. 'What a terrible thought!'

'It may interest you to know,' I remarked with icy dignity, 'that I am in a position to assist your negotiations very considerably.'

Lord Pargiter looked at Flask and myself like some ruthless eighteenth-century squire setting two fighting cocks at each other for the amusement of his village.

'Let's hear more, Mandrake,' he said.

'I must first know how far you have got here.'

'We have done very well,' said Lord Pargiter. 'Thanks to Trevor. In fact we're on the verge of a breakthrough.'

Flask gave one of his elfin grins.

'It's pretty certain,' he commented, 'that the Ruritanians will agree to resume diplomatic relations. They want it as much as we do. I think the time has almost come to produce the final inducement.'

He looked round conspiratorially. But there was little danger of our being overheard. We were seated in a secluded booth. In the middle of the room, the orchestra was making a fiendish din.

'You mean the Elphberg emeralds?' asked Lord Pargiter.

Flask nodded. I saw that my moment had come.

'Here they are,' I announced with quiet dignity.

I placed on the table the little package which had been so recently returned to me in the cathedral.

It was a delight to see the expression on their faces. They thought of Mandrake as a blunderer who made a hash of everything he touched. Now they would have to unthink those thoughts. Single handed, against appalling odds, I had got the gems through to Strelsau. How pleased the Foreign Office would be! I looked forward to the congratulatory letters, the decoration, the promotion and the glory. That would wipe the self-satisfied smirk off the face of little Mr Flask.

'These cannot be the Elphberg emeralds.' announced Trevor.

'Why not?'

'Because the real ones are in my safe at the Strelsau Hilton.'

'And how did you get them here?' I asked sarcastically.

119

'Joanna brought them in her make-up box.'

'They're awfully pretty,' commented Joanna. 'I wish I could keep them.'

I could feel the hot flush mounting on my cheeks.

'Then what the Hell have I been carrying all this time?' I asked, seized with the ghastly feeling that Flask was speaking the truth.

'A competent set of imitations,' replied Flask. 'Byfield briefed me in London.'

'What on earth was the point of that?'

'A deliberate deception plan,' answered Trevor. 'The opposition elements knew we would have to get the emeralds out to Strelsau. We made them all think you were the appointed messenger. That was the point of sending you to contact the Rassendylls in England. You were a marked man from then on, Oliver. This made them all waste their time chasing after you and your pasteboard imitations. Meanwhile, our official party was left free to fly into Strelsau airport with the real gems. Rather neat, I think. The various enemies of our successful agreement have all disclosed their hands to no avail. And we are sitting pretty in the middle.'

He beamed with content. Pargiter nodded with satisfaction. I could bear it no longer.

'I am absolutely disgusted,' I shrieked. 'The Foreign Office have behaved abominably. I was allowed to suffer under the misunderstanding that I was carrying the real crown jewels. I have consequently borne the most appalling privations, and risked torture and various grisly forms of death, in order to bring these trinkets to Strelsau. I did it, as I thought, for Britain. It was not the right way to treat a diplomatist of my seniority. I am perfectly furious and I shall make that clear to your friend Byfield when I get back to London. If I ever do.'

'Lower your voice, Mandrake,' suggested Lord Pargiter. 'We don't want to attract attention. As Trevor says, you are a marked man.'

'A human decoy,' I muttered bitterly.

'But none the worse for that,' said Pargiter cheerfully. 'You have played a valuable part in our scheme. It was you who drew the fire of the Ruritanian secret police and other aggressive factions. This enabled Joanna to bring in the real jewels unmolested. They never thought of suspecting her. I for one am deeply grateful. Buntingford and Balliol should be proud of you.'

The statesman bowed with old-world courtesy. I felt just a little better. Perhaps I could persuade him to recommend me for a C.M.G. or at least a C.B.E. These things matter in my world.

'Thank Heavens Oliver didn't have the real emeralds,' said Trevor Flask. 'We should have had a fit when he lost them.'

'Lost them?' I asked.

'You know perfectly well that you lost them at Zenda. You only got them back today.'

I felt quite appalled. How on earth had my little misfortune become known to the British delegation? It was an unnerving thought.

'What makes you think that?' I asked cautiously.

'We know,' snapped Flask. 'And you know we know. Let's leave it at that. I am not at liberty to disclose more.'

I felt distinctly glum. The odious Flask had been aware of my misfortunes all along. Why had he done nothing to help me? I had been made to look less than dignified. I felt a furious desire to get the upper hand.

'There's one thing you don't know,' I said with magisterial calm. 'It will come as a surprise. You may have the originals of the Elphberg emeralds. But I am proud to present you, Lord Pargiter, with another valuable bargaining counter which will greatly assist you in your negotiations.'

'What is that, Mandrake?'

'The Rassendyll ruby,' I said simply, placing the small envelope on the table like a conjuror's rabbit.

'Who gave you this?' asked Trevor crisply.

'Flavia Rassendyll.'

'This is another fake.'

'How do you know?'

'I understand stones. My Dad used to own a small jeweller's shop in Scunthorpe. Worked there myself for years in school holidays. This is a fairly obvious piece of coloured glass. Real rubies have a glow.'

Once again, I knew he spoke the truth. Flask would not lie on an issue like that. Besides, I had wondered all the time why Flavia should trust me with the great heirloom of her ancient family. It was only too probable that she had decided to make a fool of me.

'Bad luck, Mandrake,' said Lord Pargiter, with the air of a schoolmaster encouraging one of his weaker pupils. 'Full marks for effort though.'

'Hard cheese, Oliver,' added Flask. 'Better luck next time.'

Joanna dug me slyly in the ribs. I gave them collectively one of my icy glares. A mood of deep depression submerged me. I had struggled through to Strelsau, and all for nothing.

'I think I'll go home,' I added with dignity. 'To England, I mean.'

'A good idea,' said Pargiter benevolently. 'The pleasures of foreign travel are seriously overrated.'

'How do you propose to get out of Ruritania?' asked Trevor nastily. 'State Security are after you, Oliver. You'll never obtain an exit visa. Besides, you have other enemies, the Elphberg gang and the Easingwold circuit.'

'I am well aware of that,' I replied coolly. 'Though I'm surprised you should know so much about me. It's up to you to get me out.'

'Of course it is,' said Lord Pargiter. 'We cannot leave a Balliol man to the mercy of the local thugs. It's quite simple. Oliver shall join my delegation. That will give him diplomatic immunity. Nobody will dare to harm him then.'

In my relief, I could almost have hugged the dear fellow. What a delight it was to deal with an old-fashioned English gentleman again.

'That's just what I was going to suggest myself,' I exclaimed with delight.

'With regret, Lord Pargiter,' said Trevor Flask, 'I must advise against that course. Oliver is unfortunately too well known. The Ruritanians will have him on their black list. They may well regard him as responsible for criminal acts. To add him to the delegation list would be regarded locally as a piece of provocation. It could jeopardize the success of your negotiations. Oliver will be looked after through another channel.'

'I suppose you're right,' replied Pargiter, 'but it goes against the grain. You know how I value your advice, Trevor. You will go far.'

'And the sooner the better,' I snapped. 'Thank you so much for the comradely help. I shan't forget.'

'Don't be silly, Oliver. We both work for Her Majesty's Government.'

'Not for long, in my case,' I retorted. 'I don't expect to get out of this country alive.'

'I've just had the most marvellous idea,' said Joanna. 'It must be my lucky day, being my birthday. All we have to do is to hand over the Elphberg emeralds now to the Ruritanian Government, and let it be known publicly that we have done so. Then everybody will realize that poor dear Oliver cannot possibly have the silly emeralds. They will stop bothering him.'

I gave the girl one of my more gracious glances, indicating the possibility of further favours to come.

'At first sight that sounds a good plan,' commented Flask judiciously, 'until one remembers that our unfortunate colleague here has probably made a number of enemies in the course of his escapades. Professional strong men do not care to be foiled and fooled. Oliver has been too clever. They may be after his blood, quite apart from the emeralds.'

'All the more reason to help me,' I wailed.

'I only wish we could,' said Flask smoothly. 'But Joanna is wrong in thinking we can simply hand over the emeralds now. The time is not quite ripe, though it soon will be. Meanwhile, it will suit us all for the opposition to concentrate their attention on Oliver. That will take the heat off us. It was what the Foreign Office planned. I have reason to think that he will be all right.'

'You're not going to listen to this frightful bounder, are you, Lord Pargiter?' I burst out. 'My only hope lies with you.'

'I'm sorry, Oliver,' replied the statesman, in avuncular tones. 'You're an amusing chap. But Sir Edmund Byfield said I must always follow the advice of Trevor Flask.'

'It has been fun seeing you, Oliver,' said Trevor, 'but from now on, you had better keep well away from us until you are summoned. The delegation does not wish to get involved in your personal problems.'

'Personal problems!' I shrieked. 'My hostess was mysteriously murdered this very evening. What do you think they have in mind for me? It won't be a quick death.'

All three of them smiled at me urbanely. But I knew that Flask had swung the others round against me. At heart now they were without mercy. I was alone, in the murderous Strelsau night.

'So you're not on my side, after all,' I commented glumly.

'Only up to a point,' said Flask. 'And not in public. In any case, there are no real sides in this game.'

'It's not my idea of a game,' I retorted, 'though it may seem amusing to you.'

Only now did I become conscious of the strange performance of the gypsy band. They seemed to be getting nearer. The leading violin player and two other performers on stringed instruments had more or less surrounded our secluded table. I thought that perhaps Lord Pargiter, as a visiting dignitary, was to be treated to a special display of virtuosity, for which he would be expected to tip generously. The music was leaping louder and faster than ever before.

Only then did I notice the long black boots worn by the leader of the band. They were quite unmistakable and they chilled me with horror. For I had last seen those boots beneath the door of the confessional box in Strelsau cathedral. They belonged to the man who had murdered Dr Gertrude Markovitz.

Suppressing a scream, I raised my eyes surreptitiously from the musician's feet to his face. It was a ghastly moment. For the face that leered at me from above the violinist's generous black moustache belonged to a man I had hoped never to encounter again. A merchant of torture and death. The unspeakable Gabriel Easingwold.

'Don't look so grim, Oliver,' said Trevor brightly. 'We'll tell the Foreign Office all about you. You might well get an M.B.E.'

The gruesome plan was only too obvious now. Music was no protection against a sticky end. Just remember the fate of Don Giovanni. At any moment I was to be kidnapped in front of the very eyes of the British delegation. After that, the future would be short and nasty.

With a yell of horror, I jumped up abruptly, deliberately overturning the heavy table onto Easingwold's feet. It is the kind of thing they do so well in movies. I had a few quick glimpses that were not unsatisfying. Flask starting to mop the wine off his shirt front. Joanna clapping with childish glee. Easingwold hopping with pain and surprise. Then I dashed for the door. As I passed the player performing on the cimbalom, a type of local xylophone, I noted his identity too and gave the back of his hair a sharp tug. It was the hateful Anton. So my enemies had been all around me.

Now I was out of the restaurant, running as fast as was possible for a man of my build. Footsteps thudded behind me as I dashed into the Strelsau starlight. Where on earth was I to go now?

Even in early life, I was never athletic. Since then the years have given me a certain rotundity. It was therefore as much a surprise to me as anyone else to find myself careering at an almost Olympic speed down the narrow alley which led out of the Gay Musketeer. It is wonderful what effects can be produced by intense motivation, as I have often reminded my juniors in the Service.

Doubling round a corner I suddenly saw an open door. Hastily skipping through, I pulled it shut behind me. My pursuers had missed the manoeuvre and thudded on down the alley towards the ubiquitous Königstrasse. For a few seconds I was safe.

But they might come back. I must disguise myself at all costs. The institution in which I now found myself seemed distinctly strange. Various elderly persons of both sexes stood around in different unattractive stages of undress. The floors were elaborately tiled. Hot steam permeated everywhere. I am pretty quick on the uptake and it did not take me long to realize that I was in one of the thermal bathing establishments for which Strelsau is noted.

An attendant motioned me forward. To my astonishment, I was led firmly into a cubicle, totally undressed by two withered harridans, and then flung into a large, foaming bath, filled not with water but with hot mud. It is not an experience for which I should have volunteered in happier times. But, as I lay back in the shallow basin, covering my face completely with liquid mud except for a breathing space through the nostrils, I could not help reflecting on my good fortune in finding so perfect a means of eluding pursuit. I was happily indistinguishable from the other muddy torsos. Even Easingwold would never find me here. The bubbling mud produced a sulphurous smell which was far from pleasant, and I did not enjoy the glutinous sensation in my mouth and ears. But at least I was safe for a few minutes. Who would have expected to see beneath my muddy mass the sensitive countenance of a senior diplomatist?

The other people in the bath, all of indistinguishable sex, were camouflaged in a similar grotesque fashion. Another brown hillock moved languidly in my direction.

'Good evening, Oliver,' said a not unfamiliar voice. I nearly jumped out of the bath.

'Is it really you?' I enquired without enthusiasm, remembering our previous encounters.

'Certainly. Beneath this curious covering you would recognize well-known terrain. I am Barbara Canterbury-Cooper. And I had been expecting you.'

We lolled horizontally, side by side in the steaming mud, and compared notes.

'Are you on my side?' I asked at once.

'Of course I am.'

'So many people say that. But they never are.'

'Poor, dear Oliver. You really are an innocent abroad.'

'I've had a perfectly ghastly time. You ditched me at Zenda.'

'I tried to get you back.'

'By sending that frightful Easingwold after me!'

'He seemed so keen to help. At least it made him show his true colours.'

'You appear to know a lot, Babs. Who are you working for?'

'Britain of course. I was sent out to look after you.'

'Then you failed dismally.'

'Oh, I don't know. Just consider those apparent coincidences which really saved your skin. My people were responsible for introducing Flavia to old Gertrude, back in Hampstead. So Flavia sent you to a safe house in Strelsau. And what about that bus with the Canadian ladies? Do you really think they materialized just by chance?'

'So you were there in the background all the time. You might have let me know.'

'You had to suffer, Oliver dear. It was the only way to make the villains expose themselves. At least, I sometimes managed to keep our delegation informed about your tribulations.'

'I suppose that horse business of yours is just a front.'

'Certainly not. I am a dedicated horsewoman. And I really am working here with the State Circus. It's the greatest possible fun. But when I'm asked to do things for the country, of course I help. Daddy was in the Navy.'

'I still don't understand how you came to be expecting me here this evening.'

'Just the sequence of events. I know people in the Foreign Office are all frightfully clever. So please try to take this in. I have looked after you all along. As you may remember, I secured admission to your bedroom in the Zenda Palace Hotel.'

'I have not forgotten.'

'Wasn't it gorgeous? I'm looking forward to a repeat. It didn't take me long to find the hiding place of the crown jewels. I took them away for safety.'

'They were fakes.'

'Nobody had bothered to tell me that. Then later my contacts here saw your advertisement in the Strelsau newspaper. It was I who returned the emeralds to you in the cathedral. Of course I knew that your next move would be to contact the British delegation. I watched you meet them in the Gay Musketeer. I also saw Easingwold and his frightful crew arrive. London have been suspicious of him for years. I guessed you would have to get out in a hurry. So I made sure the door here was left open. It was the only way for you to bolt.'

'Babs, you have hidden depths.'

'Yes, there's a good deal beneath my muddy façade.'

'I suppose I should say I am grateful.'

'That would be the conventional sentiment.'

'You're an absolutely gorgeous girl.'

'What a good way of putting it. Isn't it cosy here, Oliver? Such a good spot for a workout after a tough day with horseflesh.'

'Feel free to nod. I feel quite done in.'

'You are in great danger, Oliver. I suppose you realize that?'

'I certainly do.'

127

'My contacts are sure that Easingwold murdered your friend Gertrude.'

'I know that too.'

'But do you understand why? It is part of a deliberate plan to discredit you and ruin the negotiations between the Ruritanian and British governments. Easingwold will lead the authorities here to believe that you, a senior British diplomat, have committed murder here in Strelsau. He will present it as an act of passion. It will be disastrous for the cause of *détente*.'

'But that's all nonsense.'

'Of course it is. But your enemies are very skilful.'

'I must get out, Babs. Here and now.'

'Leave it to me.'

'I shall be delighted to do so.'

'We will go and scrape the mud off each other's body. You will enjoy that. Then we will leave by the back way. I have a circus trailer round the corner. You'll have to lie in the straw at the back. I will take you to the compound of the Ruritanian State Circus. I have my own snug caravan in a remote corner beyond the horses. It will be bliss.'

'It's too late for a performance, Babs.'

'Don't be stuffy, Oliver. I'm in charge now.'

The caravan was certainly cosy. The rest of the field was in darkness. It was all very peaceful, except for the occasional animal noise. They go to bed early in circus circles in Strelsau.

'Please stop that fooling,' I said. 'I've had a terrible day.'

'Oh, Oliver, I do love you. You're such a cuddly old booby.'

'I thought our relationship was now established on a purely professional basis.'

'If you believe that, my dear, you can believe anything.'

'How on earth am I to get out of this damned country? They'll never let me through the frontiers.'

'The solution is almost childishly simple. You must travel with the Circus. The management want to please me and I can get you taken on. We leave the day after tomorrow for the German Democratic Republic. From East Berlin I can smuggle you quite easily into West Berlin and so home. Nobody bothers to check up much on circus people. We're a polyglot,

128

international lot, of no political significance. The passports are examined *en masse*. They won't investigate the occupant of each caravan. Especially the living quarters of an English lady.'

'It sounds a marvellous idea. I shall enjoy watching the acts.'

'You'll have to do more than that, my dear Oliver. To earn your keep, I mean.'

'My dear girl, you surely don't expect me to perform.'

'I certainly do. It's essential that your presence in the Circus should arouse no suspicion. Now what skills can you offer?'

'None at all, Babs,'

'You might give a hand with animals. The Great Sebastian could do with some help in his lion-taming act.'

'Certainly not. I am not at all brave.'

'It's quite easy. You just stare the beasts between the eyes.'

'That wouldn't work with me.'

'We can always use help in clearing up after the elephants. The roar of the crowd seems to have a disturbing effect on their digestive system. You just follow them round with a bucket and spade.'

'That's not quite me, dear. It would be an unusual role for a trained diplomatist.'

'You are a difficult boy, Oliver. I shall have to take you in hand. What about joining the trapeze team? Have you a good head for heights?'

'You must be joking.'

'Then only one solution is left. You will have to join the clowns. Beppo and Tonio welcome untrained support. Their sense of humour is pretty basic. And the get-up is ideal for disguise. The red nose and baggy pants will transform you completely. You'll have the time of your life.'

'I find your suggestion rather offensive.' I opined with dignity. 'You seem to be losing all touch with reality, Babs. Do you seriously expect an officer of my seniority to act the buffoon in public, just when a British diplomatic mission is in town? Suppose Lord Pargiter or Trevor Flask were to get wind of such an escapade? It would be the ruin of my career.'

'It will be the ruin of your career if Gabriel Easingwold gets hold of you again. Or the mad Earl of Burlesdon.'

'That is no doubt true. But I can prove my innocence. If necessary, I will make a clean breast of everything to the Ruritanian authorities.'

'I shouldn't rely on that. Professor Lemberg can hardly remember you with affection. You lost him his cushy billet at Zenda. He's combing Strelsau for you too. There's nothing so frightening as a gentle intellectual who decides to become ruthless.'

'You must allow me to be the final judge, Barbara. I am trained to weigh up various factors and then to reach decisions. I have been doing it for some time.'

'Don't be stuffy, Oliver. You're underrating the danger. It's not as if your tolerance of pain was exactly outstanding. By tomorrow you'll be howling for the red nose.'

'If you do that again,' I said with some asperity, 'I am more likely to need bandages and antiseptic ointment.'

I felt decidedly wonky the next morning. Breakfast in the cluttered caravan was not a lively meal.

'You were awfully rough last night,' I complained. 'All I needed was sleep.'

'Nonsense, Oliver. You're in the pink of condition.'

'Black and blue would be more accurate.'

'I've been out for hours with the horses, while you were hogging it in bed. It's a lovely fresh morning.'

'Not to me.'

'The news is bad though. One of my Ruritanian friends has read an official announcement in the newspapers. It states that a certain Dr Markovitz was murdered last night in Strelsau by a foreign spy. There is a full description of the method, as established by the police. Death was caused by a deadly new poison extracted from castor oil. A small pellet of the substance was squirted through the wire mesh in a confessional box. Collapse would have been almost instantaneous.'

'It sounds only too likely. Gabriel and Anton excel in new ways of death.'

'There's a description of the suspected murderer too. A fat middleaged man of moderate height with fair hair.'

'Could be almost anyone.'

'But there's a photograph of the suspect too. All citizens of Ruritania are asked to watch out for him. Look, here it is.'

'That does look rather like me.'

'It *is* you. You're a marked man, Oliver.'

'What on earth can it mean?'

'Easingwold and Lemberg may be working together, if only for the time being. It will suit them both to get you caught. That closes the case for Lemberg. And for Easingwold it means the collapse of the negotiations with Britain. A nail in the coffin of *détente*. You're in deadly danger.'

'Oh, do stop saying that,' I shouted testily. 'What will happen if they catch me?'

'You will face a summary trial and then a firing squad. If you are lucky.'

'I don't fancy that.'

'There is only one way out. I told you last night.'

'I don't see myself as a fall guy. If that is the technical expression.'

'It will be a novel experience for you, dear.'

'These awful clowns, will they expect a lot from me?'

'Not in the least. You leave it all to them. Beppo and Tonio are splendid characters. There's a great team spirit in this Circus.'

'Oh, all right. I agree. But under protest. The sooner I get into costume, the better.'

'You'll love the gear, dear.'

'Mind you, I'm doing this for the nation. To avoid embarrassing Lord Pargiter. But I suppose I might have some fun with those clowns.'

'It's more likely,' countered Barbara crisply, 'that they will have fun with you.'

I realized later what she meant.

I had experienced the thrill of a circus atmosphere before. The lights. The expectant audience. The heady music. But on previous occasions I was in ringside seats. Now I was in the ring myself. Under the fantastic dress, the hat, the red nose, the pallid make-up, I felt hot and confused. My air of quiet dignity seemed to go down with the crowd, who gave me a warm reception. But I felt sadly out of place.

Beppo and Tonio were small, wizened men, looking not unlike Easingwold's garden gnomes. But I had underrated the strength of their physique and their determination to amuse the mob. I had hoped to keep in the background and expose myself as little as possible. This however, was not to be. It soon became painfully apparent that I had been assigned a central role in the act, as a kind of victim or stooge. It is not the sort of role I usually play.

With an unexpected lunge, Beppo rushed towards me and flung me into the air. I felt myself propelled violently towards Tonio who was waiting for me at the other end of the arena. Between them they started a sort of surrealist badminton, using me as a human shuttlecock. No sooner had I recovered from one wild dash than I found myself repeating the process in the opposite direction. Almost sobbing with humiliation and chagrin, I felt deeply conscious of the absurdity of my position. It was too bad of Barbara to allow me to be treated publicly in so barbarous a manner. The crowd loved it all and roared their applause. Had I not been in perpetual motion, I would have responded with one of my cool stares.

Now the unspeakable Beppo and Tonio moved into a new routine. They brought on a large bucket full of red paint and started squirting it at me with syringes. I naturally tried to elude them, and there was wild applause as they followed me around with their streams of the nauseous fluid which kept getting into my eyes and hair. I attempted to quell them by my dignified demeanour, but this only seemed to provoke further mirth. In the wings I could see Barbara Canterbury-Cooper trying to conceal hysterical laughter. I would certainly give that young person a piece of my mind.

Then to my horror and disgust, I observed that the British delegation was sitting in the front row. It was an appalling discovery. They seemed to be greatly enjoying the show. Lord Pargiter was beaming merrily. Joanna's sex-starved countenance was wreathed for once in a seraphic smile. Even Trevor Flask appeared to be having fun. As I dashed past them, I could hear him speak.

'Do you see that clown in the middle?' he asked. 'The plump one, who seems so cross. You know, Lord Pargiter, he looks uncannily like that ass Mandrake.'

132

It was too much. Impulsively seizing the bucket of red paint, I flung it briskly in the direction of Lord Pargiter and Trevor Flask. My aim, for once, was satisfyingly accurate. As they mopped their astonished faces, I made a tactful retreat. The memory is one that I still cherish. It was an unusual episode in a diplomatic career which has had more than its share of ups and downs.

'Certainly I have not lost my sense of humour,' I said with asperity. 'But I have been wronged, deeply wronged. I have endured appalling hardships. I have risked ghastly dangers. And all for nothing.'

'Not for nothing, my dear Oliver,' replied the bland voice of Sir Edmund Byfield. 'You did it for the nation. And for the Service.'

'But the Elphberg emeralds were false.'

'Life is full of illusions. You played a vital part in the deception plan. As soon as we first met, I saw how useful your expansive personality could be to us.'

'As a human decoy.' I said bitterly. 'Crashing around in the undergrowth.'

'Won't you have another glass of port? They do you rather nicely here.'

For once he had invited me to Black's in St James's Street. It showed only too clearly how defensive the Foreign Office mandarin must feel at heart. No wonder, after the way he had treated me.

'There is one thing I can tell you now,' continued the great man. 'It may help. The Elphberg emeralds were never of the slightest importance. In fact the whole negotiation was a façade. The Ruritanians were desperate from the start to resume diplomatic relations. Pargiter could not have failed, however hard he tried.'

'So he was fooled too?'

'That would be one way of putting it. The truth is that the Prime Minister has been finding old Pargiter rather a nuisance in the Party. He has obstreperous ideas. A cooling-off period in Strelsau was just what the doctor ordered. It was all arranged with Number Ten at the highest level. And of course the Ruritanians were flattered.'

'Did Flask know this?'

'Certainly not. You know how seriously he takes his work. This must be between the two of us.'

He gave me a conspiratorial wink. I was beginning to feel a good deal better.

'By the way,' continued Sir Edmund, 'your name will appear in the next Honours List. It's the least we can do.'

Could he really mean a knighthood? It would be unusual in my grade. But a wild spasm of hope shot through me.

'What exactly will I be getting?' I asked.

'The O.B.E. For services to British foreign policy. You have helped most notably to incorporate the Strelsau dimension.'

Suddenly, behind Byfield's shoulder, I saw the unpleasing features of Brigadier Rassendyll moving in our direction. Bleak panic seized me. I was back in the almost ruined Castle of Elphberg, at the mercy of the mad Earl of Burlesdon.

'Ah, my dear Rudy,' said Sir Edmund, with the cordial manner he reserved for those with significant connections. 'Won't you join us for a glass of port? You already know Oliver Mandrake, I think.'

'Excuse me,' I said, rising hastily, 'I don't feel at all well.'

'It's so lovely to see you again,' said Debbie.

'I feel the same, darling.'

'You seem a bit changed since your holiday in Ruritania.'

'I've lost weight.'

'It's most becoming. But I mean more than that. It's almost as if you were – well, more quiet and gentle.'

'Gentleness is a quality I have learned to appreciate.'

After the appalling females I had met recently on the Continent, it was good to be back with a docile English girl, of rose-bud complexion, who seemed disposed to give me neither bites nor bruises. Even her dullness seemed a virtue after the extravagances of Flavia, Babs and poor old Gertrude.

'I'm so glad,' said little Debbie. 'I only want to do what I'm told.'

It was a novel sentiment and one which appealed. I gave her one of my charming beams.

'I'd like to go to Sevenoaks with you some time, Oliver dear.'

'What ever for?'

'To meet your mother and aunt.'

Instinct and long experience warned me that danger was at hand.

'I hardly think that would be possible,' I countered coolly. 'They are both recluses.'

'You had quite a time in Ruritania,' commented Lorenzo Fontwell, when I called on him in Personnel Department.

'I did indeed.'

'Well, I suppose we shall have to do something with you now.'

'That's what I came for.'

'Have you ever thought of retiring prematurely from the Service, with compensation for loss of career?'

'I have not.'

'These are days of retrenchment, my dear Oliver. You could do something quite new. Keep a pub in Devon, for example.'

'If I am retired from the Service,' I said with aplomb, 'I shall publish my reminiscences. These will include an account of my appalling experiences in Ruritania. To Hell with the Official Secrets Act.'

'I spoke only in jest. Perhaps we could use your Ruritanian experience. There's a new embassy to staff in Strelsau. The post of Counsellor there is vacant, if we could get you a visa.'

'Who will be our Ambassador?'

'Trevor Flask has just been appointed.'

'No, thank you,' I said with massive dignity.

'We must celebrate your return,' said my aunt.

'Oh, yes,' echoed Mother.

'I have already bought the tickets. I'm taking us all. It's a local show.'

'How delightful,' I said. 'What kind of show?'

'A travelling circus. They are quite a rarity in England these days.'

'A circus!' commented Mother. 'What a strange choice.'

'Oliver used to enjoy the circus. When he was a little boy.'

'Well, he isn't a little boy now.'

'I have added two more to our party,' continued Aunt Margot. 'Venetia Canterbury-Cooper used to be at school with me. I met her in the library and we had a chat. Her girl Barbara will be down for the weekend. She does some sort of hush-hush work, besides the horses.'

It was too much. There was a sparkle in Aunt Margot's naughty old eyes. Was this one of her macabre jokes?

'I love the circus myself,' continued my aunt with glee. 'Especially the clowns.'

'I feel sorry for them,' I said. 'The audience tends to forget that they are human too.'

'Some people came to look for you,' said my mother, on my next visit.

'What sort of people?'

'One was very large and didn't speak. I thought he had a nice face. The smaller man did the talking.'

'Did they leave a name?'

'They said there was no need. They left a present instead. And they promised to come back some weekend when you would be here. They seemed keen to see you again. Apparently they owe you something.'

'Where is the present?'

'Outside.'

'Outside?'

'It seemed the best place, dear.'

Mother led me out to the neat back lawn. On the grass were two strange objects.

I recognized them with a thrill of horror. Garden gnomes. Perky and Grumpy.

'Help!' I shouted, somewhat to my mother's surprise.
'Poor Oliver,' she said. 'It has all been too much for you.'